"I should have never gotten involved with this."

"You did the right thing. We both know that." Zach glanced at his smart watch. No messages. "We both know Ashley didn't leave that apartment because she wanted to, and I think you're a smart woman."

"You don't know me."

"No, I don't. I do hope you'll take my advice and find someplace else to stay until we know Ashley's safe and her disappearance has nothing to do with your meeting with a DEA agent and the suspicious activities at the clinic."

"Even if Dr. Ryan was improperly prescribing prescription drugs, he wouldn't hurt Ashley." Bridget's tone had a faraway quality. "He has two children. The oldest is in college."

"Do you think people who commit crimes don't have families?" His eye twitched. Ashley wasn't kidding when she mentioned Bridget was naive. However, he had to give her kudos for coming forward. Now he had to nudge her not to lose her nerve.

Before someone made the decision for her.

Alison Stone lives with her husband of more than twenty years and their four children in Western New York. Besides writing, Alison keeps busy volunteering at her children's schools, driving her girls to dance and watching her boys race motocross. Alison loves to hear from her readers at Alison@AlisonStone.com. For more information, please visit her website, alisonstone.com. She's also chatty on Twitter, @alison_stone. Find her on Facebook at Facebook.com/alisonstoneauthor.

Books by Alison Stone

Love Inspired Suspense

Plain Pursuit
Critical Diagnosis
Silver Lake Secrets
Plain Peril
High-Risk Homecoming
Plain Threats
Plain Protector
Plain Cover-Up
Plain Sanctuary
Plain Jeopardy
Plain Outsider
Seeking Amish Shelter

Visit the Author Profile page at Harlequin.com.

SEEKING AMISH SHELTER

ALISON STONE

LOVE INSPIRED SUSPENSE
INSPIRATIONAL ROMANCE

LOVE INSPIRED® SUSPENSE
INSPIRATIONAL ROMANCE

ISBN-13: 978-1-335-40496-1

Recycling programs
for this product may
not exist in your area.

Seeking Amish Shelter

This edition published by arrangement with Harlequin Books S.A.

For questions and comments about the quality of this book, please contact us
at CustomerService@Harlequin.com.

Love Inspired
22 Adelaide St. West, 40th Floor
Toronto, Ontario M5H 4E3, Canada
www.Harlequin.com

Printed in U.S.A.

Casting all your care upon him; for he careth for you.
—1 Peter 5:7

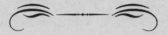

To my wonderful family, including my adult children, who all came home to keep me company while I wrote this book during the spring of 2020. It was like old times, minus car pool. Love you guys, always and forever.

ONE

The transit bus door whooshed open and dumped Bridget Miller off four stops short of home. The hum of traffic and pedestrians newly released from their downtown office jobs had become a familiar pulse these past five years that had generally energized her. Made her excited for the vast opportunity that lay ahead, especially on a Friday afternoon.

But lately, the vibe—so different from the farm she had grown up on—had a higher frequency, making her edgy and cautious. Ready to snap. And rightfully so, considering her life of school-eat-work-sleep-repeat had been upended when she stumbled upon something—possibly illegal—that made her feel uneasy at the health-care clinic where she worked while attending nursing school.

Today had been her last day of work before her scheduled vacation prior to starting her last year of nursing school ten days from now. She had saved enough money to get her through the final push. The only thing left was to report what she had witnessed.

Bridget plucked at her T-shirt, which was sticking to her on this hot August afternoon. The crowd of unfamiliar faces swirled and blended into one giant blob of humanity. Her throat went dry. *Calm down.* She drew in a deep breath through her nose and immediately wished she hadn't. A putrid smell assaulted her. She'd never be able to identify all the city smells and, quite frankly, she wasn't sure she wanted to.

She yanked open the door to a coffee shop, one unfamiliar to her. That had been intentional. She found a table for four near the back and took a seat facing the door. Her rule-following nature made her feel conspicuous taking up a table without buying a coffee. A sip of caffeine would snap her already jittery nerves. And she wasn't exactly hungry. She dug her smartphone out of her backpack and swiped a finger across the screen to check the time. She had arrived on schedule. The others were late. Ashley Meadows, her coworker, had insisted they arrive separately so they wouldn't draw attention. Besides, her friend had taken the day off, which was strange because she hadn't mentioned it. The office manager had assured her that Ashley had texted in her vacation request this morning.

Bridget's constant companions, self-doubt and indecision, twined in her stomach. Maybe she should go. But before she had a chance to bail, a man in jeans and a T-shirt strode into the coffee shop on a gust of wind that nearly took the door off its hinges, if the man hadn't had quick enough reflexes to grab the handle and yank it shut.

His intense gaze scanned the dining area, not settling on anything or anyone in particular. He was handsome in the "my T-shirt fits snugly over my firm pecs and my five o'clock shadow darkens my square jaw" sort of way. He was the kind of guy Ashley would have called dibs on, as if the two college-aged women had control over such matters. Well, maybe Ashley did. Bridget chose to focus on more serious things, like school and work.

Bridget's hand twitched. Should she wave him over? No, he seemed too casual to be with the DEA. Then again, what did she know about law enforcement? About any of this? If it hadn't been for Ashley, who'd set up this meeting, Bridget would never have had occasion to meet with an agent from the Drug Enforcement Administration. *Ugh.* The nausea clawing at her throat made her wish she could rewind the clock and say no to this ridiculous plan.

Her conscience would never allow her to ignore what she suspected Dr. Seth Ryan, the clinic director, was doing at the clinic.

The man she was watching made directly for the counter and placed an order. It seemed he wasn't the agent she had been waiting for. Her shoulders sagged at the momentary reprieve, and she returned her attention toward the front door again.

Come on, Ashley. Where are you?

Once Ashley got here, Bridget wouldn't be forced to figure out what to say to the agent on her own. She checked her phone. The throbbing pang of uncertainty roared in her ears. *Be in this world, not of this world.* God had wanted her to be in the healing profession—she knew that with every fiber of her being. Had He wanted her to get involved with this? A health-care fraud investigation? Despite learning about fraud in her college classes, she had never thought she'd be part of something like this. Wasn't that exactly why they discussed these topics in class? So that they'd be knowledgeable?

Bridget twisted her fingers in her lap. Reading about it in a textbook was one thing—meeting with a DEA agent was entirely another. She had never met someone in law enforcement in person. Her childhood had taught her to stay separate. God's law above man's law. Yet God wouldn't want her to look the other way on this.

What if she was wrong?

What if innocent people were hurt by her accusations?

Biting her lip, she stared at the blank phone screen. *Still* no message from Ashley. She couldn't possibly have gotten cold feet. Or had she? Something about how all these events had unfolded had bothered Bridget from the beginning. When Bridget confided in Ashley, she was the one who'd initially suggested Bridget look the other way when it seemed Dr. Ryan had ordered a prescription for a controlled substance for a patient who had died the previous month from complications due to diabetes. After all, the middle-aged doctor had been good to his employees. He was beloved by his patients. He had run the clinic for longer than Bridget had been alive. He certainly wasn't getting rich from running an inner-city clinic.

That was the first thing that niggled at the back of Bridget's brain.

Her instinct was to go to the doctor—who had forgotten to log out of the computer—and tell him he had made a mistake, but she feared he might wonder why she was using his computer. She had slipped into his open-door office when the computer that the nurses shared had locked up. Then curiosity made her return a few times to see if it was a one-off.

It wasn't.

When Bridget could no longer ignore her concerns, Ashley had warned her that the physician might not take kindly to the accusation, but she'd ultimately suggested they contact Agent Zachary Bryant, a childhood acquaintance, hoping he could look into it. According to Ashley, audits of controlled substances were standard practice, and this way no one would have to know they'd made a report.

It all seemed logical. Easy. Ashley had called Agent Bryant a few weeks ago, and because of work-related obligations, today was the first time he could meet. A heaviness weighed on Bridget's chest, making her claustrophobic in the crowded café.

Where is Ashley?

"Bridget Miller?" A deep voice made her jump. The handsome man she had watched wrestle the door into submission was staring down at her, holding two coffees in his hands.

"Yes?" she responded hesitantly.

He slipped into the seat across from hers, and a ghost of a smile touched his lips. "Special Agent Zach Bryant." He kept his voice hushed. "I thought you might like some coffee." He slid one of the cups across the table and tipped his head toward a counter along the wall. "Cream and sugar are on the stand."

Bridget placed her hand on the plastic lid and dragged the cup closer. "This is fine." She was too polite to tell him otherwise. "Thank you."

The DEA agent peeled off the lid of his coffee and dumped in three sugars and stirred the drink with a wooden stick. He took a sip and studied the room with sharp brown eyes. "Where's Ashley?"

"I don't know." The plastic lid made a satisfying sound under Bridget's fidgety fingers. "I'm hoping she's just late. She hasn't responded to my texts since last night."

He seemed to regard her thoughtfully over the rim of his cup while he took another long sip. "Should we start without her?"

"Um, yeah, I guess." She hated how timid she sounded. She had worked hard over the years to shed the submissive nature that had been bred in her since childhood. She squirmed in her seat before catching herself, squaring her shoulders and giving the agent a confident, "Yes, let's start." Reflexively, her gaze drifted to the door.

"Ashley told me you have concerns at your place of employment?" The agent shot a furtive glance over his shoulder toward the door, then around the café. Nearby patrons seemed too engrossed in their own business to be paying much attention to theirs.

"Yes." Bridget's heart felt like it was going to beat out of her chest as she recounted how she'd first discovered prescriptions for deceased patients.

"How long ago was that?"

"Um…" Bridget swallowed hard. "Two months ago."

"And you're reporting it now?" The agent's stern glare sent a sheen of sweat coursing across her skin.

She bit back another "um" and forced herself to return his steady gaze. "To be fair, you've been hard to reach. Ashley insisted we wait to talk to you."

The agent seemed to settle back in his seat. "Tell me what you know."

"About two months ago, I borrowed my boss's computer. I saw a prescription for a deceased patient that caught my eye." She pressed her lips together and considered how to frame this. "I hesitated to report this immediately because I was afraid it could have been a misunderstanding, and Dr.—" she stopped herself short since they were speaking in public "—and if I accused the doctor and I was wrong, I could cause him a lot of problems." And, as selfish as it sounded, she didn't want to lose her job over a false accusation.

"But you're convinced now?" The hint of doubt in his question made her stomach bottom out.

Bridget's gaze moved over his shoulder toward the door. "How much did Ashley tell you? Does she think I'm wrong?" The slow sting of betrayal worked its way up her spine. Had Ashley purposely left her to respond to this agent's inquiry on her own? Was Ashley leaving her to take the fall in case she was totally wrong about the doctor's activities?

No, no, Ashley had been a loyal friend.

And Bridget wasn't wrong.

"I don't want to get into specifics in a public venue. Ashley told me about your concerns after you used your employer's computer. Tell me your thought process on this."

"People make honest mistakes. I really wanted to believe that was the case. The doctor works hard. He seems tired." Bridget rubbed the bridge of her nose, and her eyes burned. The agent sat silently, apparently waiting for her to continue. "However, a patient of mine—an older woman— told me last month that her son overdosed on drugs that are readily prescribed by physicians. I know sometimes these same drugs are prescribed fraudulently because there's a lot of money to be made." Bridget pushed the coffee toward the center of the table. The thought of it made her stomach flip. "I couldn't look the other way. If the doctor at the clinic is involved with anything unethical, he needs to be stopped."

The agent seemed to consider this for a moment. "Unfortunately, there's a lot of this going on. Do you know if the doctor has had any money trouble?"

"I don't know."

"Okay." The agent took the last sip of his coffee and stuffed the wrappers from the sugar packets inside the cup.

Bridget looked around at the unfamiliar faces and kept her voice low. "I understand the DEA audits clinics for compliance. That perhaps I wouldn't have to get involved."

The agent seemed to regard her a moment. Then he pulled out his cell phone and tapped out something with his thumbs.

The reality of what Bridget was doing hit her. Dots

danced in the periphery of her vision. "The doctor seems like such a good-hearted person. He helps low-income patients. He's waived their co-pays. Recently, he's been caring for the homeless." She knew how naive she sounded. People weren't always what they seemed.

How did I get involved in this mess?

The agent looked up from his cell phone. "Have you noticed any other unusual activity?"

"After my patient told me about her son's overdose, I did some searching on the internet about how—" she threaded her fingers, then twisted her hands "—about how people get drugs." She shook her head, realizing she probably sounded ridiculous. She plowed forward anyway. "We seem to have a lot of repeat patients, and we do have a pharmacy on site." Shrugging, she felt her face growing red. "I could be seeing what I want to see. Since I didn't want to do anything unethical in case I was wrong, I confided in Ashley, and she told me she knew someone who investigated these types of things." *Stop rambling.* She checked her phone again. Still no Ashley. "Will you look into it?" Hope made her voice squeak.

"I'll take the information to my office and see when we last audited the location. The DEA is very stringent on the requirements to make sure there are no violations of the Controlled Substances Act." The agent stood and picked up his cup. He obviously had better things to do. "I'm currently on…" He seemed to be about to say something, but then changed his mind. "I'm on vacation now. I just came off a rough case. I'll hand off your complaint."

"Hand it off?" The band around her chest that had been easing grew tighter. She'd have to explain herself again?

The agent lifted a shoulder as if to say, *Whatcha gonna do?* He ran a hand over his short brown hair. "Does anyone other than you and Ashley Meadows know about this?"

"No one." Bridget pushed to her feet, and her chair bumped into the half wall behind her.

"Keep it that way." His solemn note made her shudder. He handed her his business card. "I'll inform my supervisor. She'll be in touch."

"Okay." Bridget would be lying if she didn't admit to herself that she was upset that Ashley's handsome friend was passing the case off.

"If there is fraudulent activity, the perpetrators aren't going to be happy to be shut down. There are a lot of violent people involved in drug trafficking."

"Drug trafficking. That's not…"

The agent lifted his eyebrow. "Just because a person has an MD after his name doesn't mean he's any less guilty of trafficking drugs than the gangs and cartels."

"Can I drop you off somewhere?" They stepped outside the coffee shop, and Zach turned to Bridget The late-afternoon sun cut across his line of vision, and he slowed to slide his sunglasses on. He had a bad feeling about this young woman's report, and he was rarely wrong. Bridget was obviously a bright woman who would recognize inconsistencies in prescriptions, but he feared her naivety would make her a prime target. He let out a long breath. And Ashley Meadows being a no-show nagged at him. He had confirmed their appointment yesterday afternoon after having the worst day in his career.

"No, thanks. I don't live far." She smiled up at him, a weary look on her face he had seen on a number of innocent bystanders who had gotten wrapped up in something they never in a million years thought they would. "I could use the fresh air." She flicked her hand in a wave and started toward the intersection.

Zach scanned the faces of the pedestrians filling the

sidewalks. *Where are you, Ashley?* His former neighbor had claimed she had changed, but her absence today brought back a lot of hard feelings. When Ashley had called him about her coworker's concerns, she had painted Bridget as a wide-eyed nursing student who had grown up out in the country. He had gotten the distinct impression Ashley had wanted to control how and where Bridget made a report, and to perhaps convince her that her concerns were invalid. Or maybe Zach was being too hard on Ashley. He still hadn't forgiven her for the role she had played in his sister's death.

Don't go there. You've got enough going on without delving into old hurts.

Zach did another quick check of his phone to see if Ashley had called. *Nope.* It seemed Bridget, walking away with her head dipped, was doing the same thing. Debating if and where he should grab some dinner before going home, Zach hesitated and watched the commuters surge forward at the intersection. The crosswalk beacon flashed red numbers: thirteen…twelve…eleven… If he hustled to the corner, he could make it. He slid his phone into his pocket and broke into a jog.

A car revved its engine, drawing Zach's attention. A bright blue muscle car with tinted windows flexed its impatience. He rolled his eyes, then checked the signal. Five… four… He stepped off the curb. He'd make it across easily.

"Excuse me, sir." A gentle tap on his arm made him stop and look down. An elderly woman who came up to his elbow tugged on an unmoving two-wheeled metal pull cart. "The wheel is stuck. Can you help me?"

"Of course." He grabbed the side of the cart and lifted it up and out of the narrow grate slit. "There you go."

"Thank you," the woman said, then she squinted at the traffic light. "Sorry, I made you miss the light." A black SUV whizzed past, confirming that they had indeed missed their chance to cross.

"No problem." Zach guided the woman back up onto the curb, then pressed the button to cross. The next surge of pedestrians crowded in around them. On the other side of the road, Bridget waited to cross the next street. Based on the tilt of her head, she appeared to still be distracted by her phone. Zach noted the muscle car idling in the far-right lane, its engine revving. *How obnoxious.* The side windows were tinted, making it impossible to see the offender. Probably some twentysomething trying to impress with a car and its payment that forced him to live in his parents' basement.

Across the way, pedestrians stepped off the curb to cross, and Bridget trailed behind. Just then the idling car shot forward, its tires squealing as it made a sharp right turn directly into the crosswalk.

A woman screamed.

Cars screeched to a stop.

Horns blared.

Zach's heart lurched. He ran into the street, slapping his open palm on the hood of the closest car to get the driver's attention. Thankfully the car had slowed to a crawl due to the commotion. With a job as an undercover agent, he knew one of these days, things weren't going to go his way. Until then, he'd keep taking chances.

Was that what he had done with his CI? Taken too many chances? Now the poor kid who'd been giving him key information on some drug dealers higher up in the chain was dead. No redemption for that kid.

A horn blared, and Zach reflexively held out his palm and then jabbed his index finger in the general direction of the impatient driver. By the time he reached the crosswalk, a crowd had gathered, making it impossible to see what had happened. He scanned each face. *Where's Bridget?* The roar of the muscle car grew distant, weaving around cars and disappearing down the street.

"Excuse me, excuse me…" Zach pushed his way through the gawkers. When he reached the center of the crowd, he found a young man crouching down next to a seated Bridget. Her pink face indicated she was either in pain or embarrassed, possibly both. Thankfully, she was conscious. Talking. Relief washed over him. He touched the man's arm. "We're good here. Thank you." The man stood, nodded and walked away.

Bridget's eyes brightened with recognition. "I had the right of way in the crosswalk."

He took her elbow. "Are you okay to stand? Let's get you out of the street."

"Yes. Thanks." He helped her to her feet. Bridget shuddered, as if shaking away the cobwebs. "I know better. I should pay more attention." She lifted her hand, still clutching her smartphone. The other palm had bits of gravel embedded in it. The crowd had begun to disperse. Apparently, a walking and talking victim didn't have the rubbernecker appeal of a chalk outline on the pavement. In his rush to check on Bridget, Zach had made a tactical error. Any witnesses to the near miss had been swallowed up in the crowd.

He guided Bridget to the corner restaurant's outdoor dining area that spilled out over the sidewalk. "Sit." A waiter came by and set down a glass of water without saying anything. "Are you okay?" Zach asked.

Bridget pulled up her skirt and examined a scrape on her knee. She studied her red palm before looking up sheepishly. "I think I'll live." She silently picked the pieces of gravel out of her palm, then gently rubbed her hands together.

"Did you see the car? The person behind the wheel?"

A tiny line furrowed her brow. "No. I heard the loud car, turned my head and barely had time to jump out of the way. I lost my balance and fell."

"The car didn't hit you?" Zach asked, doing a quick top-to-bottom assessment of Bridget.

"No. I'm fine. Really."

"Do you know anyone with a bright blue muscle car? Maybe someone who hangs around the clinic?"

Her brow furrowed. "I don't even know what a muscle car is." She shook her head. "I don't know anyone with a bright blue car, either way." Her eyes grew wide. "You think that was on purpose?" She scooted to the edge of the seat, making like she was about to stand. "I need to go."

"Wait. Have a drink of water."

Bridget took a sip, then set the glass down. "I'm fine. I want to go home." Worry clouded her pretty brown eyes.

Rubbing the back of his neck, Zach considered how the car had idled on the side of the road before gunning it around the corner. It felt too coincidental. "Are you sure no one besides Ashley knows that you were going to meet with me today? Perhaps someone overheard you two talking at work?"

Bridget lifted her hand to her throat. She'd be clutching pearls if she were wearing them. All the color drained from her face. She lifted the glass to her lips, and a splash of water landed on her lap. "No one knows. We were careful." The spark of defiance in her eyes lacked conviction.

"Someone could have tracked your computer usage."

"I was careful." Bridget slid the glass away from her, and the water sloshed over the sides. She stood, wobbled and grabbed the back of the chair. "No one knows except Ashley."

Despite her assurances, he wouldn't leave her safety to

chance, even if he was officially on leave. A forced vacation, really. "I'll drive you home." Zach scanned the crowd again, grumbling to himself that he hadn't had a clear view of the license plate.

She pinned him with her gaze. "I'm perfectly fine to walk."

"Humor me."

Bridget tilted her head, and a long strand of silky brown hair fell into her eyes. She absentmindedly dragged it out of her face with her pinkie. Her nails were short and unpainted. "Fine, if it will make you feel better."

He hiked an eyebrow and stifled the grin that was forming on his lips. "It will make me feel better. I'm parked in a nearby lot. You okay to walk?"

"I *said* I could walk." A spark of indignation flashed in her eyes. She gathered her long brown hair over one shoulder and raked her fingers through it. A nervous tic. The faint freckles on Bridget's nose grew more pronounced on her peaked face.

Zach suspected the hard edge to her tone was more from fear than annoyance. Like her, he wanted to believe that some cocky driver had taken a corner too fast with complete disregard for the pedestrians in the crosswalk. His gut told him otherwise. This near miss felt more like a warning.

First Ashley's a no-show. Now this. His gut was rarely wrong.

TWO

Zach hesitated for a moment with his hand on the gear-shift of his pickup truck before he pulled out of the down-town lot. "We need to find Ashley."

"Now? Do you think she's in trouble?" Bridget searched his face, his concern mirrored in her eyes.

"I'd feel better if I talked to her."

Bridget tucked a strand of hair behind her ear. "My sister's in town and staying at my place. She'll wonder where I am if I don't get home by a certain time, Agent Bryant."

"Call me Zach. You okay if I call you Bridget?"

"Yes, sure." She smoothed out the fabric of her skirt over her thighs. This young woman dressed more conservatively than most women her age. He found it charming.

"I feel like maybe we got off on the wrong foot in the café."

Bridget shrugged.

"I can come off gruff. I'm used to dealing with…" he tipped his head "…all sorts of people who you probably wouldn't want to bring home to your parents." He gave her an apologetic smile, and she rewarded him with one in return. One of her eye teeth was slightly crooked. Again, charming. He shook his head to dismiss the distracting thoughts. Maybe he really did need this leave. He *was* getting soft. Losing his edge.

"And I'm sorry I snapped when you offered me a ride home." She balled up her hands in her lap, then straightened her fingers to check out her scuffed palm. "This is so far out of my comfort zone. Dr. Ryan is such a nice guy." She gently brushed her fingers across her palm. "I can't imagine why he'd get involved with something like this." Her lips thinned into a grimace. "Do you think he paid someone to hurt me?"

"My office will look into it."

Bridget leaned back on the headrest and turned to face him. "Your office? I know you said you were on vacation, but can't you look into it?" Her soft voice washed over him. He wanted nothing more than to say yes, but it wasn't his call. He had been told in no uncertain terms that he had to take some time off. He had a strong feeling that he was at a pivotal time in his career, and this leave wasn't a request.

"I recently came off a rough case." He cleared his throat, picking his words carefully. "I was asked to take leave."

"I don't understand what that means."

"I guess you could call it standard protocol when things don't go exactly right on a case." He wasn't about to tell her someone died because of his recklessness.

Bridget rolled her head to look out the passenger window. "I'm sorry, I assumed…" She looked back in his direction. "I shouldn't have done that. Obviously, you met me as a favor to Ashley." He wondered how much Ashley had told him about their history. About her friendship with his sister. "Now what? You give me the name of someone else in your office?"

"Well, let's hold off on that. What I'd like to do first is check on Ashley. Can we do that real quick? Then I'll get you home." He ran a hand roughly over his jaw. He hadn't been clean-shaven in months, and he was still getting used to the stubble. "Maybe call your sister. Give her a heads-up that you're going to be late."

"I can't call her. I don't have her number." Her monotone made it hard to determine if she was being sarcastic.

Zach made a noise with his lips and pulled out of the city parking lot. "You know where Ashley lives?"

"I don't know her address." Her eyes brightened. "But I can show you. I've been to her house." She shifted in her seat. "Turn right here." Bridget tugged on the strap of her seat belt. "Ashley never told me how she knew you," she said. "Oh, wait, turn here."

"Ashley was a friend of my sister's when they were in high school." That's all Bridget needed to know. His little sister's bright blue eyes flashed in his mind's eye. He hadn't seen her beautiful face in over seven years. He had been stationed in the Middle East when he got the call that she was dead.

"Did they have a falling-out? Oh, wait—" Bridget pointed toward the street on the left. "Turn at the stop sign."

Zach turned, happy to avoid the question. "Is her house on this street?"

"Yes. There." Bridget pointed to a neat double on the right. It had two entrances.

Zach pulled his truck up alongside the curb. It didn't appear that anyone had followed them. Four years as a DEA agent did that to a person.

They climbed out of the truck and approached her apartment. "Her unit's on the left." Bridget checked her phone again.

"Still no word?"

"No." Bridget looked up at him with worried eyes. "This

is so unlike her. She's one of those people who responds to texts. Always."

Zach knocked on the front door. Deep inside somewhere, a dog barked. "She have a dog?"

"The neighbor does." She pointed to the window next door. A lace curtain danced in time with the frantic jumping of what Zach's mother used to call a yippy dog. Everything annoyed his mother.

"I'm going to walk around the outside. See if anything looks out of place."

Bridget crossed her arms and cupped her elbows. For a fraction of a beat, Zach wondered what her story was. All he knew about her was what he'd gotten from Ashley—Bridget was a nursing student working as a nurse's aide at the clinic. She had a look of innocence about her that made him wonder if she'd get beaten down by the demanding nature of nursing. The job had eaten his weak-willed mother alive and had destroyed their family.

He scrubbed a hand across the back of his neck and turned his attention to a car approaching. Easier to throw himself into work than deal with his own demons. A vehicle that had traveled the salted streets of more than a decade of winters pulled into the driveway.

A female driver on the plus side of sixty took her sweet time and finally emerged with a bundle of Target bags in both hands. "Can I help you?" she asked, curiosity more than wariness rounding her eyes.

"Do you live here?" He pointed to the unit next to Ashley's.

"Yes. Who wants to know?" She transferred one of the plastic bags to free up a hand.

Zach dug out his credentials and flashed them at her. Most people didn't check them out; this woman proved the exception and squinted, drawing closer to check out his ID. "DEA? What's going on?" Her pale eyebrows rose above the thick frames of her glasses.

"I'm looking for your neighbor Ashley Meadows. When was the last time you saw her?"

The woman's Target high went poof, and her features grew pinched. "Did something happen to her?" She pointed to her excited dog at the window. "Barney was barking at something last night around midnight."

Next to him Bridget sucked in a breath.

"Did you happen to look outside when your dog was barking last night?" Zach asked, wondering if he'd catch a break.

"Only caught a pair of headlights pulling away." She adjusted the plastic bags again. "Not sure if that's what had my Barney all wound up or not. Listen, I need to put these bags down. I'm sorry I don't have more information for you." The woman awkwardly fished for something in her purse while juggling the bags. If Zach hadn't been so anxious to locate Ashley, he would have offered to carry her bags in for her.

"Are you her landlord?" Zach asked. Maybe she'd have keys to the apartment.

"No, someone else owns the house. We both rent." The woman frowned. "I *really* need to get these things inside."

Zach tipped his head. "Please, go. Sorry to keep you. Thanks for your time."

"Never a dull moment," the older woman muttered as she stepped up on the stoop and unlocked her front door.

Zach scanned the street. "Does Ashley have a car?"

"Yes." Bridget frowned and looked around. "I don't see it."

"Well, let me take a walk around the property." Zach brushed his hand on Bridget's elbow. "Maybe you should wait in the truck."

"I'd rather stick with you, if that's okay."

"Sure." Zach's pulse roared in his ears, his naturally honed radar on alert. Something was definitely off here. "Do me a favor and stick close."

They circled the garage and crossed the back lawn, a few weeks past due for a cut, unlike the tidy front yard. He stepped up on the concrete back patio, and Bridget followed. Each unit had a single door leading to the patio. A few dirty white plastic chairs were arranged in a circle. Perhaps Ashley had had some friends over. The vertical slats of the blinds covering the neighbor's back doors moved, revealing a more subdued Barney. Perhaps with his master safely inside, he was more intrigued by the strangers than concerned.

"What are you looking for?" Bridget asked, rolling up on the balls of her feet.

"I want to make sure nothing's out of order."

Bridget crossed her arms again and trembled.

Zach reached for the handle on the back door, twisted it and muttered when it popped open. He pivoted and locked gazes with Bridget. "Stay here." He reached for his gun strapped to his ankle under his jeans. With one hand, he pushed the door open wide, and with the other, he aimed his gun into the heavily shadowed apartment of Ashley Meadows.

As she stood in Ashley's backyard, Bridget's legs wobbled, and the blue sky and green trees went monochromatic. She dragged one of the white plastic chairs closer to the dirty siding and sat down. Her stomach threatened to revolt, and she was grateful she hadn't drunk that coffee Zach bought her at the café. She closed her eyes and tried to calm herself.

God, please let Ashley be okay.

A lifetime of her father's, the bishop's, the entire Amish community's warnings about staying separate from the evils of the outside world rang in her ears. Fortunately for her, she wouldn't have to see them gloat, because she wasn't welcome in her hometown of Hickory Lane. Either way, it wasn't in their nature to gloat. The goal had been to strike fear in the hearts of the youth so that they'd never leave. However, Bridget's passion had overridden their caution, and look at her now. Bouncing her legs with nervous energy while a DEA agent searched her friend's apartment.

Oh, why did I stick my nose into someone else's business? I should have done my job and gone to school. Today was my last day at that clinic anyway... Please, please let Ashley be okay.

Bridget tucked the folds of her skirt under her thighs, then pulled out the fabric and smoothed it. Her stress had exceeded the heart-racing, mind-scrambling, nausea-inducing levels she'd experienced the night before she jumped the fence and left Hickory Lane.

Look how that turned out.

Self-doubt had a way of ramping up her worst fears.

Bridget stood and shook out her tingling hands. A moment later, Zach appeared in the doorway. He had holstered his gun and concealed it under his pant leg. "Ashley's not here."

"No?" Her squeaky voice could barely be heard above her thrumming pulse. Was that good or bad?

The intensity in his eyes suggested the latter. She stepped inside without taking his offered hand. He closed the door behind them, trapping them with the stale scent of day-old garbage and something Bridget couldn't quite identify.

"I need you to tell me if you notice anything missing."

Bridget scanned the room, taking in the little details

of Ashley's life: a sweatshirt tossed aside, a pair of shoes kicked off, dirty dishes on the counter. "I don't know."

Zach walked toward the back hallway. "How about in her bedroom?"

Bridget slowed. "Her bedroom? Aren't we invading her privacy?"

"We need to find Ashley." When Bridget didn't immediately respond, Zach added, "She'll understand."

Zach palmed the door to open it all the way. Ashley's bed was unmade, and one sneaker was upturned on the hardwood floor. Perhaps the other one had been kicked under the bed. Zach gestured to the closet with his chin. "There's not a lot of clothes." He pulled open a couple of drawers in the only dresser. "Not much in here, either."

The whooshing in Bridget's head grew louder. "Do you think she took off somewhere?"

He tilted his head as if considering. Why would Ashley have taken off when they had plans to meet the DEA agent? Bridget walked out of the bedroom and went into the bathroom. She didn't know what she was looking for—maybe proof that her coworker had left on her own. Bridget had made up for lost time after growing up without a TV—she'd watched her fill since moving to Buffalo. Didn't bad guys stuff clothes into a suitcase to make it look like their victim left?

Bridget tugged on the edge of the bathroom mirror. Zach lingered in her peripheral vision. It opened with a click, revealing a medicine cabinet. She picked up a prescription bottle. "Allergy meds." She put them back in the cabinet.

Zach leaned on the bathroom door frame. "How well do you know Ashley?"

"I met her my sophomore year in an advanced biology class. She recommended me when there was an opening at the clinic. We've worked together for about two years." Bridget knew a nonanswer when she heard it. How well did she really know Ashley? "She wouldn't just up and go. I know that." Wouldn't her Amish neighbors have said the same thing about her? How many hearts had she broken when she ran away in the middle of the night?

Bridget brushed past Zach on her way to the family room. Everything seemed mostly where it should be. "Ashley wasn't really neat, so it's hard to know if anything is out of place." She twirled a long strand of her hair around her finger, then let it drop. She was about to ask Zach for his take when a black object poking out from under the couch caught her attention. She bent down and scooped it up. She palmed the weight of the cell phone, and the screen lit up revealing all the missed texts, mostly from Bridget.

Where are you?

You're late.

Is everything okay?

Bridget's hand began to tremble. Everything was definitely not okay. Behind the text bubbles, her eye was drawn to the wallpaper image: a selfie of Ashley and Bridget sticking their tongues out with Dr. Seth Ryan in the background throwing double peace signs. A crack that had splintered across the screen distorted the image.

Bridget handed the phone to Zach, fighting back her growing panic. "Ashley would never have gone anywhere without her phone."

THREE

"Come on—we have to go." Zach pocketed Ashley's cell phone and took Bridget by the elbow, ushering her toward the back door leading to the patio, where they had come in.

Bridget swung out of his grasp and glared at him. Disbelief and fear flashed on her pretty face. "Where is Ashley? We have to find her."

"We'll talk in my truck." He had to get Bridget to safety. *Now.* Ashley Meadows's apartment wasn't the place.

"We're going to leave?" Bridget held out her palms, indicating Ashley's apartment. "Maybe there's a—" she seemed to be searching for the right word "—clue or something here. Aren't you trained in this sort of thing?"

"I do have a plan." Zach needed to get her moving without panicking her. "Once we're in my truck, I'm going to reach out to a contact in the Buffalo Police Department. He'll come back here, make sure it's secure and interview the neighbors. Okay? Let's go."

This time Bridget hustled around the side of the house with Zach keeping her close, hyperaware of his surroundings. Nothing seemed out of place in this tranquil neighborhood. The tires on his truck squealed when they pulled away from the curb. He made the promised call to his buddy, Freddy Mack, of the Buffalo PD. His time at the

DEA had him working closely with officers of various law enforcement agencies, including Freddy. When he ended the call, Bridget whispered, "Please take me home now."

"Is there someplace else you could stay until we locate Ashley?"

She shrugged. "No. My sister is visiting. I have to go back to my apartment."

"Listen…" He made a quick decision to zip onto the expressway without signaling. He kept checking his rearview mirror. No other car seemed to be following him. Perhaps he was being paranoid.

Bridget leaned forward and slowly lifted her thumb. "I live back—"

"I need to make sure no one is following us before I take you home." He checked all his mirrors again. Nothing suspicious. If Bridget wanted to go home against his advice, she had to know what she was potentially up against. "I'll drop you off and go back to Ashley's apartment to investigate myself, if that's what you want. However, we don't know what we're dealing with. Maybe you almost getting run down and Ashley disappearing are both major coincidences and have nothing to do with your meeting with a DEA agent." She had to realize the potential danger she was in. "You're welcome to get on with your life and hope for the best if that's what you want." Never in good conscience would he actually let her do this.

"Of course I want to get on with my life." Her tone was harsher than he'd expected. "I reported what I saw at the clinic because it was the right thing to do." Bridget released a long sigh and looked up. "I should never have gotten involved with this." Some of the fight seemed to be draining out of her.

"You did the right thing. We both know that." Zach had no idea what they were dealing with. "I can't make you do anything. What you do next is up to you." He glanced at his smartwatch. No messages. "We both know Ashley didn't leave that apartment because she wanted to, and I think you're a smart woman."

"You don't know me."

"No, I don't. I do hope you'll take my advice and find someplace else to stay until we know Ashley's safe and her disappearance has nothing to do with your meeting with a DEA agent and the suspicious activities at the clinic."

"Even if Dr. Ryan was improperly prescribing prescription drugs, he wouldn't hurt Ashley." Her tone had a faraway quality. "He has two children. The oldest is in college."

"Do you think people who commit crimes don't have families?" His eye twitched. He blamed the caffeine. Ashley wasn't kidding when she'd mentioned Bridget was naive. However, he had to give her kudos for coming forward. Now he had to nudge her not to lose her nerve.

Before someone made the decision for her.

Zach pulled into the busy parking lot of a superstore. He put the truck into Park and met Bridget's gaze squarely. "I've been a DEA agent for four years. I mostly work undercover." He pressed his lips together and shook his head, trying to shut out the gruesome images he'd seen on the job. "Please let me take you and your sister somewhere safe for the night. We can reevaluate the situation in the morning once we locate Ashley. Please."

Bridget ran her thumb over her bruised palm, seeming to be working something out for herself. "I don't want my sister to know what's going on." She looked up at him with wide brown eyes.

"I'm willing to go at this any way you want." He raised an eyebrow, waiting for her to continue.

Bridget threaded and unthreaded her fingers. "My sister, Liddie, is supposed to go home tomorrow. I wish she had already left." She seemed to be thinking out loud. "I can't have her reporting this back to my family."

"Do you have a friend you both could stay with? Someone not associated with the clinic?" He didn't want the bad guys to find their safe house.

Bridget shook her head. "I'm busy with school and work. I don't socialize much."

"Anyone from school?"

"Not really. Ashley's my closest friend." The knuckles of her clutched hands grew white. "Do you really think we won't be safe at the apartment?"

"Something went down at Ashley's place, and she's missing. I don't want to sit back and wait for you to go missing, too."

A shudder seemed to rack Bridget's small frame. Her silky hair fell forward and hid her face. After a moment, she lifted her head and stared at him. He didn't know her well enough to read her mostly blank expression. "I can probably spring for a cheap motel for the night for me and my sister. I'll frame it as a girls' getaway." She twisted her lips, as if the lie pained her. "And you're a friend from work who kindly offered to give me a ride since I don't own a car and all that." She blinked slowly, perhaps surprised at how quickly she had come up with a cover story. "She can't know what's going on or that could put her in jeopardy, right?" The lilt of her voice suggested she was looking for his approval.

"You're making the right decision." He put the truck in Drive again. "Now tell me, where do you live?"

"Can't you wait in the truck?" Bridget turned to stop Zach from following her across the parking lot to her second-story apartment.

"I'm sticking close."

"Hmm…" Bridget mentally rehearsed the cover story for her sister. Lying wasn't part of her nature. This was about protecting Liddie. About protecting both of them. Having Zach hanging over her shoulder wouldn't help.

If this horrible day *had* to happen, Bridget wished it could have waited twenty-four hours. Her sister would have been home in Hickory Lane and none the wiser. The last thing she needed was for Liddie to tell her parents how royally her big sister had screwed up in the big, bad outside world. This fiasco would only prove her conservative Amish parents' point—it was better to remain separate.

A hot flush washed over her as she reached the stairwell.

I've done far scarier things in my life. I can handle this.

Oh, man… How much longer could she give herself this pep talk? She picked up her pace, her hand skimming the railing and her full skirt tangling between her legs. "Liddie!" she called when she opened the apartment door. She strode through the small apartment to the spare bedroom, where her sister's things were neatly piled in the corner. She must have started packing.

"That's strange." She met Zach back in the living room. "She's not here." Her mind flashed back to Ashley's empty apartment, and a surge of panic rolled through her. Then a bright yellow Post-it glowing on the kitchen counter caught her eye. Bridget read the note and sent up a silent prayer of thanks. "Ah, she's down by the pool."

"Text her. Tell her to come up," Zach said.

"You're forgetting I don't have her number." Bridget bristled at his authoritative tone. "She owns one of those cheap disposable ones." Liddie picked it up when she arrived, claiming she wanted to chat with her other friends who had either smuggled a phone into their Amish homes or were also currently on *Rumspringa*. Funny thing, Bridget never broke the rules when she was living at home. She bided her time and broke the ultimate rule.

"The pool is in the courtyard. It'll take me two seconds to get her."

"I'm coming with you," Zach said, and Bridget didn't bother to argue.

They left the apartment, and Bridget locked the door behind them.

A familiar laugh caught her attention when she reached the thick green hedge surrounding the pool. Her sister. Bridget let out a relieved breath that she hadn't realized she'd been holding. She paused, partially hidden by the thick screen of bushes, and held up her hand to stop Zach. "Hold up," she whispered. She wanted to see who her sister was talking to. Despite having left Hickory Lane five years ago, she automatically felt protective of her younger sibling.

Liddie was sitting on a lounge chair wearing the only pair of jeans Bridget owned and one of her college T-shirts, her legs crossed under her. She looked like every other *Englisch* twenty-one-year-old. She was twirling her hair and flirting shamelessly with a young man, probably about her age, who wore a baseball cap pulled down low over his forehead, shadowing his eyes. This kid wouldn't know what hit him when her sister disappeared as suddenly as she had appeared. Bridget's stomach flipped. Her sister had better not tell him she was Amish. Former Amish. That was a secret Bridget kept from everyone. It was easier to say that she was from farm country. That usually stopped people in their tracks. People weren't curious about farmers. Long ago, she had grown tired of being the object of curiosity of tourists who flooded her small hometown to see the Amish, as if they were some sort of reenactors there

for their entertainment. She didn't want to bring that kind
of scrutiny upon herself unnecessarily.

"We have to go." The urgency in Zach's voice, whispered close behind her, made goose bumps race across her
arms. She still couldn't wrap her head around the idea that
she was in danger. *What did you expect, silly girl?*

"Stay here." Bridget touched the back of his hand and
was surprised by how smooth it felt. Her eyes lifted to
his, and something stretched between them. Inwardly she
shook her head. *There's nothing there. He's just doing his
job.* "Please, stay here."

"Hurry, please." Zach gave her a subtle nod.

"Hey, Liddie." Bridget spun around and pushed down
the latch on the security gate and entered the pool area,
plastering on her best "nothing going on here" smile.

"There you are." Liddie leaned forward. "You're late."
Her sister untucked her legs and planted each bare foot on
either side of the lounge chair and wiggled her toes. She
must have painted her toes pink when Bridget was at work.
"This is my friend Jimmy. We've hung out at the pool a
few times when you're at work."

"Hi, Jimmy," Bridget said politely, aware of Zach lurking behind the hedge where he couldn't be seen. Ordinar-
ily, she'd feel protective of her sister hanging around some
random guy, but today she was feeling protective for completely different reasons.

"Hello." Jimmy pulled his cap down lower.

"Sit down, join us," Liddie said. "Jimmy got here a few
minutes ago when I was trying to get a shot of that cute
chipmunk we saw the other day. Remember how cute it
was?"

"I'm afraid I made dinner plans for us and don't have
time to sit down," Bridget said, pointing with her thumb
in no particular direction. "Excuse us?"

"Yeah, no prob." Jimmy crossed his tattooed arms over his chest and settled in, apparently content to soak up the last of the evening sun.

"We have dinner plans?" Still sitting, Liddie held up her hand to shield the sun from her eyes. "Wait, what happened to you?" Leave it to her little sister to recognize immediately when something was wrong. Bridget must have made a face, because Liddie added, "Your hair is messed up and..." Liddie scooted to the edge of the lounger, and it tipped precariously under her weight. Surprise flashed across her face, then she giggled and adjusted her position. The back legs of the lounger clattered against the cement. Liddie pivoted and scooted off and stood. "Are you okay?"

Bridget played with her skirt, grateful its length hid the scrape on her leg.

Liddie pulled up the fabric of Bridget's skirt, revealing the angry red mark. "What happened here?"

Heat pulsed off Bridget's entire body. "I'm fine. I stumbled when I was crossing the street. I wasn't paying attention. It was stupid."

Liddie frowned and flipped her hair over her shoulder. She had become an expert hair flipper during the short time that she had been here, considering she had to wear her hair neatly tucked under a *kapp* in Hickory Lane. "You're the least clumsy person I know."

Bridget shrugged. "I'm fine. Let's go in." She made eye contact with Zach, who peeked out from behind the shrub. He jerked his head impatiently toward the apartment.

"So, dinner, huh? Where are we going?" Her little sister's enthusiasm was contagious.

"Hey," Jimmy called, "did you want me to send you that photo?"

"Oh, yeah." Liddie giggled. She jogged over to Jimmy. They chatted for a few moments while Bridget waited impatiently. She could feel Zach's eyes boring into the side of her face. When Liddie came back, she said, "He got a cool photo of that chipmunk." She waved her hand. "Anyway... you sure you're okay?"

Bridget smiled tightly. "I've had better days." She cleared her throat. "I thought maybe we could have a girls' night before you go home. Let's go upstairs and talk about it." She pushed on the gate and held it open. Zach stood on the other side of the hedge, drawing the women up short.

Liddie was about to walk around him when Bridget said, "And this is *my* friend Zach."

"Oh..." Liddie seemed to shake her head to clear her confusion. "You have friends?" *Leave it to Liddie.*

"Ha-ha." Bridget forced a smile. "I'm full of surprises."

"Apparently." Liddie rolled up on the balls of her sneakers. *Bridget's* sneakers. "Nice to meet you, Zach."

"This is my sister, Liddie."

"Nice to meet you." Zach greeted her sister, his gaze constantly sweeping the courtyard. Another chill raced down her spine. Did he think someone had followed them here?

"Are you cold?" Liddie asked with disbelief. "You'd think that long skirt would keep you warm." Her sister had playfully harassed her about her business wear, claiming it was one short step away from the Amish dresses they wore growing up. Bridget would be the first to admit she didn't have much business savvy. She thought a long skirt and conservative top were safe choices. She saved her most casual clothing for home. Or for Liddie to borrow.

Bridget rolled her eyes. "Let's go upstairs. I want to tell you about our plans. Zach said he'd drive us."

"Oh, cool." Her sister's eyes screamed, *Nice going, sis.*

Bridget jogged up the stairs, suddenly very eager to get inside.

"What's the rush?" Then, perhaps sensing the vibe, Liddie asked, "What's going on? There's something you're not telling me."

Zach brought up the rear and ushered them inside. "We should probably get moving."

Bridget clenched and unclenched her hands, suddenly unable to think straight. She cleared her throat, and a warm flush spread across her cheeks. "Zach's going to drive us to a hotel. We can order takeout, watch TV and veg before you have to go home tomorrow. Won't that be fun?"

Liddie narrowed her eyes, studying her. "I smell a fish. What's really going on?"

Bridget caught Zach's attention. He didn't offer any help. "I thought it would be fun to stay in a hotel," she quickly added.

"You act like I've never stayed in a hotel."

Bridget bit her lower lip, afraid she wouldn't be able to convince her sister to leave without telling her the truth. For some reason Bridget was especially determined that Zach not find out that she had grown up Amish. *Why does it matter, really?* Perhaps because she had spent the past five years doing her best to keep her past in the past. To break out and live a new life.

"Remember the time *Mem* and *Dat* took us to Niagara Falls?" Liddie asked, still not making any effort to gather her things.

"Yes, of course. We can order room service and movies. Then you can catch the bus home tomorrow." Bridget opened the closet by the door and grabbed her sister's jacket. Bridget was hoping she could shuffle her sister out of Buffalo tomorrow morning, none the wiser of what was going on in her life.

Liddie took the spring jacket from her sister and draped it over the back of the couch. "What's the rush? Oh, I suppose your friend has plans. Zach, are you in a hurry, too? Do you have a date?" Liddie was not a wallflower. Once she got herself into trouble with their father because she refused to apologize for beaning the schoolyard bully with an apple from her lunch. She claimed he deserved the whack and not an apology. Man, Bridget had missed her younger sister. Well, mostly. She'd have to get her back for this.

Bridget's face was on fire. "Stop harassing my friend. Let's go. I'm hungry." Well, she should be hungry. She hadn't eaten since breakfast. The knot in her stomach made it impossible to eat.

"Room service, huh?" Liddie asked, a flash of excitement in her eyes.

"Burgers, maybe?" Bridget was really going to miss her sister. She had no idea if she'd ever see her again—well, for more than a brief visit. She still couldn't believe their parents had allowed her to come for a visit. Even though Liddie enthusiastically answered all of Bridget's questions about their family and life back in Hickory Lane, her sister had never once tried to convince Bridget to come home.

"Let's go so we can take advantage of the time we have left," Bridget said, the band easing around her lungs as her sister finally started picking up her personal items strewn around the living room.

"I'll pack an overnight bag." Bridget locked eyes with Zach, who nodded slightly.

"How did you and my sister meet?" Liddie picked up the book that she had been reading from the table next to the couch.

"He's a friend from work. Now hurry up," Bridget called from the hallway.

A loud crash sounded on the other side of her closed bedroom door. Her heart exploded, and her pulse roared in her ears. Panicked, she spun around. Zach was on her, apparently in full DEA agent mode. He firmly shoved her behind him. With the palm of one hand on the door, he turned the handle with the other. Thick smoke poured out, and he slammed the door shut. "We've got to get out of here. Now!"

FOUR

"Go! Go! Go!" Zach checked the landing outside Bridget's second-story apartment and hustled the two women out the door.

Liddie turned to grab something, and Bridget pulled at her arm. "We've got to go!"

He scanned the area outside the landing again, his eyes stinging from the black smoke. Whoever had set the apartment on fire couldn't be far. He pounded on each door as he passed and yelled, "Fire!" He didn't slow to see if anyone came out. He couldn't leave Bridget exposed.

Bridget and her sister got ahead of him when they reached the parking lot. He aimed the key fob at his truck and hollered, "Get in! Get in!"

Bridget spun around, and Zach followed her gaze above the roofline. Black smoke pumped out from her apartment on the far side of the building. She blinked, seemingly snapping out of it, and ordered Liddie to get into the truck. As naturally protective of Bridget as he was—it was his job, after all—she was equally protective of her sister, perhaps more so.

Bridget climbed into the passenger side after helping Liddie get into the back seat. Once Zach was behind the wheel, he called 9-1-1 on his smartphone, which was connected by Bluetooth to his vehicle. "There's a fire at…" He tipped his chin toward Bridget and asked, "Address?" On cue, Bridget hollered her address, holding firmly to the grip bar as he pulled out of the parking lot, made a sharp left and raced down the road, all while constantly checking his rearview mirror.

"I have the occupants of the apartment with me. I'm taking them to safety." Zach gave Dispatch his name and badge number to confirm he was a DEA agent. "Make sure the building is empty. I had to get my witness to safety."

Once Dispatch assured him that Fire Rescue was on the way, he ended the call. "Now do you have any doubts you're the target?" He hated his sharp tone, but he was not going to let this poor, naive woman be a sitting duck because she didn't want to believe her decision to speak up had put her in harm's way. He checked his rearview mirror again. The road was quiet. Liddie sat wide-eyed and silent. He made a quick right, then another left, keeping his foot pressed on the pedal.

Zach cut a sharp gaze over to his passenger. All the color had drained out of her face. A dark smudge marred one cheek. He didn't want to think about what would have happened if she had been in her bedroom when whatever it was that set the room on fire came crashing through the window. He should have taken her directly to his office, made a full report. He should not have let her go back to her apartment.

"Are you okay?" Zach eased off the gas. They were safe. For now.

"What am I going to do?" High-pitched alarm made her voice squeak.

Her sister leaned forward in the back seat. "What in the world is going on? I'm going to guess Zach here isn't a friend from work." Despite the seriousness of the situation, a hint of excitement laced her tone.

Bridget shook her head tightly and seemed to be at a loss for words.

"I'm a law enforcement agent. Your sister reported—"

"Stop." Bridget finally spoke up. "Liddie doesn't need to know everything."

"Um, Liddie's right here."

Bridget shifted in her seat to look at her sister. "You can't tell *Mem* and *Dat*." Zach had a hard time placing her accent.

"I think they'll wonder why I've returned home with none of my things." In the rearview mirror, he watched her pluck at her T-shirt. "I don't have my plain clothes."

Plain clothes?

"We can stop to pick some up before you go home." Bridget lifted her chin in determination. "You have to go home in the morning."

"Where's home?" Zach asked.

Bridget lifted her hand in a silencing gesture. Liddie ignored her. "Hickory Lane."

"Where's that?"

Bridget sagged into her seat and tugged on her seat belt. "Hickory Lane is about an hour from here. It has a large Amish community."

"Amish?" Zach nearly sputtered out the word before he had a chance to consider his audience. He cleared his throat. "Did you grow up Amish?"

Bridget ignored his question. "Liddie is going home first thing in the morning. It will draw more attention if we were to drop her off tonight."

"I can't go home without making sure you're okay. And you're definitely not okay. Someone set your apartment on fire," Liddie said. "I may not be worldly, but I'm not stupid."

"I never said you were stupid." Bridget's tone softened. "I can't deal with all of this. *Please*."

"Tell me what's going on," Liddie pleaded. "What did you report?"

"Take us to the hotel." Bridget tilted her chin, as if that settled everything.

"Fine, we'll go to a hotel, but I'm not going home until you tell me what's going on." In the rearview mirror, Zach watched Liddie cross her arms tightly over her chest.

"I'll figure it out. My classes start the week after next." Bridget shrugged. "Maybe I can get temporary housing through the university."

Zach was done holding this tongue. "I need to make sure you're someplace safe until we figure out who's targeting you."

"Isn't that obvious?" Bridget shook her head. "Someone knows I was meeting with you." She fidgeted with the seat belt. "Shouldn't someone go find Dr. Ryan?"

"The doctor you work with?" Liddie asked, obviously confused.

"All that will have to be investigated," Zach said. "Until then, you need to be tucked away someplace safe."

"Bridget, you have to come home. *Please*," Liddie begged. "You'll be safe there."

"I'm not going home." Bridget shot her sister an unmistakable "stop talking" glare.

"*Dat* and *Mem* will be happy to see you. They will, I promise." Liddie was nothing if not persistent.

"The only way they'll be happy is if I return for good." Bridget shook her head. "That's not happening. I told you I have school next week. It's too far to commute."

Zach felt like he was intruding on a conversation he shouldn't have been privy to.

"Humor me," Zach said. "Do your friends in Buffalo know where home is?" Ashley had mentioned something about Bridget growing up on a farm somewhere.

Bridget's face grew pink. "No one knows where I grew up, and I'd like to keep it that way."

"Is there a reason why you couldn't go there for the week, at least?" Zach suggested.

"Okay, here's the deal. I grew up Amish. My sister here is on *Rumspringa*. She's going home tomorrow. *Alone*. I never told anyone about my background because it lends itself to questions." She must have read something on his face, because she pointed at him. "Like that." She shook her head; frustration slanted the corners of her mouth. "It was a huge sacrifice to leave my family, and returning to Hickory Lane to stay with them is not an option. And if they learn that some evil *Englischers* are trying to…" she seemed to change course midsentence "…hurt me, they'll never let the rest of my siblings out of their sight forever." She dipped her head and scratched her forehead. "There's no winning here."

Before Zach had a chance to question her more, his cell phone chimed. "It's my contact in the Buffalo Police Department. I need to take this." He pressed Accept on the controls on the steering wheel. "Hey, Freddy, before you give me any updates on Ashley, I need to let you know you're on speakerphone. I have a friend of hers in my vehicle."

"Sorry, no updates. Still canvassing the neighborhood," Freddy said, his tone direct. "We put out an alert for her car. Wanted to keep you in the loop." The officer cleared his throat. "We'll keep looking."

"You should know that someone set Ashley Meadows's coworker's apartment on Spring Street on fire," Zach said.

"Heard the call go out on that one. Looks like someone tossed a Molotov cocktail through the window. Everyone okay there?" Freddy asked.

"Yeah, I'm taking the occupants to a hotel." Zach tapped on his steering wheel. "Let me know if you hear anything else?"

"Of course. Seems you're right in the middle of some serious stuff."

"Afraid so." Zach slowed at the red light and took notice of his surroundings. Nothing suspicious. "My office will be involved in the investigation, for sure, but we could use the BPD's eyes and ears." He hoped his supervisor agreed with him, since he was technically on leave after the Kevin Pearson incident. An incident he'd never be able to forget. Or forgive himself for.

"Sure thing," Freddy said. "Be careful."

Zach ended the call and his phone immediately rang. It was his supervisor, Assistant Special Agent in Charge Colleen McCarthy. She wasn't going to be happy.

"Agent McCarthy," Zach said into the phone by way of greeting.

"I hear you're not exactly taking it easy." The ASAC had sent him on leave.

"Just have a few things to take care of for a friend." Zach smiled tightly at Bridget as she fidgeted with her hands in her lap.

Colleen's deep sigh filled the interior of the vehicle over the Bluetooth speakers. "How important is this?"

"Life and death."

Silence stretched across the line before his boss finally said, "Agent Bryant, you're technically on leave and what you do on leave is your business. But if this blows back on the department, you'll live to regret it."

"Thanks." He understood her need to cover her backside.

"You won't be thanking me if you don't get cleared to come back to work."

"That won't happen," Zach said curtly. He was about to state all the reasons he didn't need this leave in the first place, but he had already lost that argument.

"Don't let it. Take care of your personal business and lay low. Got it?"

"Got it," he said as he turned on his directional for the hotel.

Zach ended the call just as they pulled up under the porte cochère of the hotel. "Looks like I'm cleared to help you."

"Didn't exactly sound like that to me," Bridget said in an even tone, turning to study the two-story, nondescript hotel.

"You don't know my boss like I do." He smiled. "Let's get you both inside. Then I'm going to go see what the good doctor has to say."

The next morning Bridget woke from a fitful sleep. Her nerves were humming in time with the loud AC unit on the wall of the dank hotel room. Her life had been turned upside down yesterday. Reporting her concerns to law enforcement had been worse than she could have possibly imagined. After much discussion with Zach last night, Bridget had decided she had no choice but to go back to Hickory Lane.

Bridget had no home and limited funds, which meant limited options. She prayed they'd be able to find whoever set her apartment on fire. Then, maybe she could find housing on campus and start her classes in a little over a week, as planned. The ache in her stomach told her it wouldn't be that easy.

Zach had warned her. Depending on how deep Dr. Ryan had gotten involved with his alleged prescription fraud, the drug-dealing networks were complex and had long tentacles. How was she supposed to know what she was getting into? *Ugh...*

She closed her eyes briefly and sent up another prayer for Ashley. When she was done, she rolled over and plumped up her pillow and settled her head back down, not quite ready to start the day. Would she ever be ready? Across the narrow space separating the double beds, Bridget found her sister watching her.

"Guder mariye." Good morning. Liddie had her hands tucked under the pillow, and her eyes shone bright in the soft light spilling in around the heavy curtains that hadn't been pulled all the way shut. For her little sister, yesterday's tragedy meant her big sister was coming home. It was a bright side to an otherwise awful day. For Bridget, it was more awfulness. It wasn't that she didn't love her family. She loved them dearly, but following her dreams meant severing ties completely with her loved ones. Going back would only tear open those wounds. Wounds she had worked hard to heal over the course of five years.

Would she have it in her to leave a second time?

"I'm not so sure it's a good morning," Bridget muttered.

The mascara Liddie had been experimenting with yesterday was smeared under her eyes. She pushed up on one elbow, and her long, loose hair fanned out over the pillow. "Maybe this is a sign." Bridget had told Liddie about the discrepancies in the prescriptions. That perhaps Dr. Ryan had been part of a pill mill. She had come across that term during her internet search. About how she finally summoned the nerve to report the well-loved doctor after she learned about a patient's son who had overdosed on this very same class of drugs.

Bridget grunted and sat up. "A sign?" The AC unit clicked off, and the room grew still. "A sign that I'm supposed to return to Hickory Lane for good?" The comforter slipped down, exposing Bridget's bare arm, and she shuddered. "Do you think this is God punishing me for leaving?" All the thoughts swirling around her brain came spilling out, directed angrily at her sister, her poor, sweet sister who had no idea how hard Bridget had worked to get this far. On her own.

Liddie smiled sadly. "We've missed you. That's all. I've been praying that Ashley is found safe. And I'm worried about you. Don't be mad at me."

Bridget's shoulders sagged. "I never meant for any of this to happen." She swung her legs around and climbed out of bed. "*Dat* isn't going to want me in the house unless I submit to God and the Amish ways in front of the community. You know that."

"Maybe once your friend explains the situation, he'll understand," Liddie said, sitting up and raking her fingers through her tangled hair.

"The DEA agent is not my friend. I met him yesterday." Bridget picked up an elastic from the bedside table and pulled her hair back into a high ponytail.

Liddie's lips flattened. "Really? Yesterday? I got a different vibe. He was all protective of you." She waggled her eyebrows. "I think he likes you."

"Oh, silly girl. That's his job." Bridget secretly took pleasure in her sister's observation. "He has no interest in me other than keeping me alive." A worldly man like him would never look twice at a simple girl like her.

"We'll see," Liddie said, laughing.

"Stop. Ashley knew Zach from her childhood. Since he works for the Drug Enforcement Administration, she suggested we meet with him." She waved her hand in dismissal.

"And still no word from Ashley?" Liddie asked, growing somber.

Bridget grabbed her cell phone from the desk. "No messages." With her free hand, she flung open the room-darkening shades in an effort to dispel the gathering sense of doom surrounding the whereabouts of her friend.

"Zach will find her," Liddie said, offering her encouragement.

Bridget sat down on the edge of the bed. "When we get home, please let me tell *Mem* and *Dat*." This was her way of grasping onto the last bit of control.

"What should I say?" Liddie asked. "I can't stand there like a dummy."

"I'm not asking you to do that. Maybe leave out the bit about my apartment?" Bridget's posture sagged. She turned, rested her chin on her shoulder and locked eyes with her sister. "That won't work, will it?"

"Might be hard to explain why I don't have any of my things."

"The truth is best," Bridget said, resigned.

Liddie flung the covers off her legs and crawled over to kneel on the bed next to Bridget. "Once you're home, it'll be like old times."

"That's what I'm afraid of." Bridget patted her sister's hand.

"Elijah and Caleb will be so happy to see you. We've all missed you."

Dread and longing twisted in Bridget's stomach. "They must have grown so much." Elijah was only eleven and Caleb seven when she left. She had resisted asking Liddie too many questions about her brothers prior to now, knowing that it would make her more homesick. However, today, she'd get to see them. "Elijah must be running wild himself nowadays. He's sixteen."

"He's a good kid." Liddie vibrated with excitement, making the mattress bounce. "They'll be so happy to see you."

"What happens when I leave again?"

"Maybe you'll change your mind." Liddie sounded so hopeful that it made Bridget more bummed.

"You have to get that idea out of your head. I have a good life here. I am going to graduate with my nursing degree next spring."

Liddie squeezed Bridget's hand. "You're coming back with me to Hickory Lane today. That's what counts."

Bridget jerked her head back, not quite sure what to say. She couldn't blame her sister for not feeling the same sense of apprehension. She didn't know Ashley. Her whole life hadn't been turned upside down. Before she had a chance to formulate a response, Liddie gave her sister a quick peck on the cheek, then bolted off the mattress toward the bathroom.

"Beat ya," Liddie said before closing the door. The shower curtain hooks scraped across the metal pole and the faucet knobs screeched a fraction of a second before the old water pipes hummed to life.

Bridget released a strangled laugh. Leave it to Liddie. Bridget flopped back on her bed and tried to quiet her mind. She was going home. To Hickory Lane.

FIVE

Bridget's family home was an easy drive west on the Thruway and another thirty minutes on back country roads south of Fredonia, New York. Zach had never explored this part of Western New York and had never heard of the small town of Hickory Lane. In the back seat, Liddie kept up her friendly banter until Bridget's silence made it evident that she wasn't in the mood for small talk.

Their first stop was a store in the center of the small town of Hickory Lane. The women needed new clothes. Zach waited in the truck. When the sisters reemerged, he had to blink twice. Bridget was almost unrecognizable in her bonnet, gray dress and black boots.

Bringing her here for safekeeping had been a brilliant idea.

"All set?" Zach asked when they both climbed back into the truck.

"Yes," Bridget said tersely. "Go straight and I'll let you know when you need to turn."

"Will do." Zach pulled away from the curb.

"What is your plan once you drop us off?" Bridget asked. "How long before I can head back to Buffalo?"

"I don't have any answers."

"I thought you made some phone calls last night." Bridget tapped her fingers nervously on the door.

"I did. The doctor's wife claims he left on a golf outing yesterday after work and isn't expected home for a few days." Mrs. Ryan had been fuzzy on the details of her husband's sudden trip, either purposely or unintentionally. Zach didn't want to believe she knew what—if anything—her husband was up to. "An agent in my office is actively tracking him down."

"And once your coworker finds him?"

"You realize it's not that simple." Zach slowed behind an Amish buggy. "Like I mentioned yesterday, it's unlikely that he acted alone." He sensed she kept asking the same question in hopes of getting a different answer.

"Bridget can stay in Hickory Lane as long as she needs to," Liddie said optimistically from the back seat.

Bridget groaned. "If I stay, you'll let me know the minute I can come back to Buffalo? Classes start a week from Monday."

"Of course." He rested his arm on the ledge of the open window and followed Bridget's directions. Fields of corn swayed in the light breeze. The last time he had been out in the country, it had been to raid a meth lab in a doublewide. Drugs had no socioeconomic boundaries.

"There," Liddie said from the back seat. "The house is the first one on the right."

A well-maintained wood structure sat between a field of corn and trees. A dirt driveway ran back toward a red barn. Flower beds interrupted the luxurious green lawn. Apparently, the Amish took pride in their homes, or at least the Miller family did.

"Pull over on the side of the road. My father won't appreciate having your truck on his property," Bridget said, her voice soft. "We can get out here."

"I'm not going to drop you off and leave," Zach said. "I need to make sure you're settled."

Bridget anxiously played with the folds in her long skirt. He followed her gaze out the front windshield. Someone dressed exactly like Bridget and Liddie was in the side yard pinning laundry to a clothesline. A row of matching pants and shirts flapped in the breeze on a parallel line.

"I'll be safe here. No one knows about my Amish roots. I made sure of that." A flash of defiance sparked in her brown eyes. "There's no need for you to stay. You can reach me on my phone when you've taken care of everything." She lifted up her smartphone, and the sunlight glinted off the screen, momentarily blinding him.

"Do you have a place to charge that?" he asked, feeling the full weight of Liddie's uncharacteristic silence in the back seat.

"I'll figure it out." Bridget slipped it into the brown bag holding the clothes she had changed out of.

Zach smiled at Liddie over his shoulder. "Would you mind giving us a minute?"

"*Yah*, of course. It was nice to meet you," Liddie said, her voice softer than it had been earlier. Perhaps the change in clothing had altered her personality somehow.

Zach smiled. "You too. Take care."

"Wait for me at the bottom of the driveway. I don't want to greet our parents alone," Bridget said, the panic evident on her face.

The woman hanging clothes had now lifted her hand to shield her eyes to get a better look at the vehicle. He didn't have long before they'd have company. "I don't think you understand how much danger you're in."

Bridget's eyes sparked with anger. "I don't?" She practically spat out the words. "Do you think I'd uproot my life, put on this dress and return home because I'm in the mood for new scenery? I *know* what's going on, and I need you to fix it. That's why Ashley said we should call you. She said you could discreetly find out what was going on. That everything would be okay." Tears filled her eyes, and the words that she had obviously been holding back filled the small space between them.

"I'm sorry everything went south." Of course, Ashley would think he could make everything okay. Growing up as neighbors in the University District of Buffalo, Ashley and his sister had been inseparable since they met in kindergarten. A million times over his little sister had come to him for help and he took care of things—a flat bike tire, an empty belly, the bully on the playground. Until he deployed and left his little sister to figure things out on her own. She hadn't been able to get a handle on her drug problem alone. He'd never forgive himself for leaving her with their mother, who couldn't take care of herself, much less her daughter.

Zach shook away the memories crowding in on him. He may not have been there for Leann, but he was here now. If he knew one thing well, it was his job. His job. He didn't exactly have that, right now, did he?

Through the rear window, Liddie could be seen pacing, her arms crossed tightly over the bib of her dress. "Please don't be upset. We only met yesterday, and I know you have no reason to trust me." He cleared his throat. "But you need to trust me. I have a lot of resources at my disposal." The only people he ever trusted were people he worked with. "Dr. Ryan is only part of the problem. Once he's in custody, there will most likely be others."

"That only sounds a little bit reassuring." Bridget rubbed her neck, then dropped her hand. "I didn't mean to be rude." Pink blossomed across the fair skin of her cheeks. "This is very stressful."

"I understand. No need to apologize."

"Okay," she announced, seeming to have come to a decision. "I need to go. My mother won't linger by the wash line forever." Two rows of laundry flapped in the wind. Her mother had gone back to pinning identical brown shirts to the remaining line, shooting curious glances over her shoulder. "If my parents agree to let me stay, will you go? Your presence won't he welcomed." She laughed, a woeful sound. "I won't exactly be welcomed, either, but at least I'm dressed the part."

"Is there a hotel nearby?"

"You're kidding me. You plan to stay in town?" She held out her palm. "I've never told anyone I'm Amish. How would they track me down here?"

"I'm not going to take the chance."

Shaking her head, Bridget pushed open the door, climbed out and slammed the door. She walked up the driveway with her sister, and her new black boots kicked up a cloud of dust. From the back they could be twins.

Zach had handled all sorts of situations in his line of work: the dealer who tried to jackrabbit on him only to be hung up on the top of a barbed-wire fence, the time a woman threw her baby at him when they raided her apartment and the shootout at the pharmacy when the zing of a bullet whistled past his ear.

He suspected Miss Bridget Miller was going to prove to be equally challenging, in her own stubborn way.

Bridget and Liddie's *mem* watched them approach, hands fisted and full of clothespins. A riot of emotions— shame, nostalgia, overwhelming love—heated Bridget's face, and she found herself fidgeting with the strings of her bonnet. She'd never thought she'd be back in Hickory

Lane, not dressed in plain clothes. What would she tell her family?

This is such a bad idea.

Stepping back onto her family's farm had been like returning to her childhood. Nothing had changed since she left five years ago. Nothing had changed in a hundred years, for that matter.

The crisp scent of cornstalks, the fresh country air, the earthy fragrance—all felt like home.

Bridget stopped abruptly and grabbed her sister's arm, panic setting her skin on fire. "I can't do this." It would be too hard to leave again.

Liddie smiled and patted her hand reassuringly. "*Yah,* you can. I'm here. And *Mem* is waiting. She'll be *so* happy to see you. You can't turn around now. You'll break her heart."

Memories from Bridget's childhood rolled over her, some happy, some not. The most tumultuous time was the year, months, weeks and days leading up to her secret departure. She had been fraught with indecision. One of the hardest parts about leaving the Amish was not being able to say goodbye to her family. That's not how it worked. When a person left, they left. No goodbye. No *I'll see you when you're in town.* None of that. Otherwise they would have talked her into staying. *Guilted* her into staying.

"Okay," Bridget finally whispered. A conscious effort to relax did nothing to ease the knot tightening between her shoulder blades. Next to a clean blue dress billowing in the breeze, her mother tossed the clothespins in the basket and slowly lifted her work-worn hands to her mouth. Tears glistened in her eyes. Bridget's heart softened. *"Mem."* The single word came out on a squeak.

"Wilkum." Welcome. Her mother held out her hands. Bridget fought the urge to run into her mother's arms and

accept the warm homecoming, not wanting to give the older woman false hope. Her mother's heart had been broken. She couldn't do that to her all over again. It wouldn't be fair. *"Wie bischt?"* How are you?

"Ich bin gut." I am well. An automatic reply from her childhood in a language she hadn't used since she left. A rush of adrenaline made her grow dizzy. She took a step backward. "This was a mistake," Bridget whispered so only Liddie could hear. Behind her, the sunlight reflected on the windshield of Zach's truck. She couldn't see him, but she felt his gaze. She was trapped between her past and an uncertain future.

"You're home." Her mother's soft voice washed over her. So familiar. Soothing. The woman who had cleaned her scrapes, wiped away her tears, first made her love the idea of taking care of others.

"*Mem*, Bridget needs a place to stay," Liddie said. "I told her she should come home." Her sister plowed forward, needing to explain, not giving *Mem* a chance to say no, and trying to keep Bridget from fleeing to the getaway vehicle sitting a hundred-yard dash away. Even if their gentle mother welcomed her home, their father wouldn't be quite so quick to forgive. Not unless Bridget asked for forgiveness. Returned to the Amish ways and followed the rules of the *Ordnung*. Another wave of emotion made Bridget's stomach flip.

As if on cue, a deep voice bellowed from behind her. "What's going on?" *Dat.* "Why is she here? This is unacceptable."

Bridget fisted her hands, bracing herself as she turned around. Her father's dark gaze, glaring out from under his straw hat, pinned her. A look so familiar, she still saw it in her dreams—nightmares. A thousand emotions rained down on her, taking her back to her tumultuous teenage years when she still believed she had no choice but to accept the Amish ways and give up her dreams of becoming a nurse. Tears threatened, and she clenched her teeth. She would not cry in front of her family. She couldn't give them any ammunition to suggest she was sorry. That she was wrong.

Was she?

Was her current mess of a life a reflection of all the bad choices she had made? Was God punishing her?

She felt her sweet *mem*'s gaze on her. How she loved that woman. Then she locked gazes with her sister. "I can't do this." She grabbed the fabric of her long skirt and ran toward the truck, forcing back the threatening tears. As she approached the truck, she tore off her *kapp*. She reached for the passenger handle and yanked the door open. She couldn't read the expression on Zach's face, dark like her father's, and something else…

"I'm not staying." Bridget climbed in, reached behind her and yanked the seat belt forward and clicked it in place.

"You have to." His tone was even, ominous.

"I can't. Go." She leaned forward and tapped on the dash, like she used to slap the hindquarters of Honey, the family's American Saddlebred. When he didn't move, she added, "Please." Her mind whirled. "Take me back to Buffalo. I'll reach out to the university. Maybe they can find a spot in the dorms for me. They might be open already. Right?" When he still didn't move, she shifted in her seat, her brow furrowed. "What are you waiting for?" She didn't bother to hide her frustration.

"You have to stay." He held out his smartphone. "A call came in."

Zach reached for her hand, and she pulled it away. If he couldn't comfort her, he couldn't give her bad news, right? As she clutched her hand to her chest, dread spread across her skin, making her feel like she had downed three cups of coffee on an empty stomach. Finally, she was able to force out a single word: "Ashley?"

"Yes." His warm brown eyes radiated his hurt. "They found Ashley near the bike path."

Bridget's brow twitched. "She liked to run there." Her phone had been smashed in the apartment. "I told her it wasn't safe." This had nothing to do with running alone. "Is she…?" She pressed her fist to her mouth in a feeble attempt to stop the overwhelming emotion welling up inside her.

No, no, no. Ashley's fine. She's fine.

Zach reached for her wrist and pulled her fist away from her mouth. He tilted his head. A sad smile slanted his lips. Every movement, every moment, marked time.

This moment.

An eternity.

Before and after.

Her shoulders sagged, and she slumped into the seat.

"Bridget…" Zach slid his hand up from her wrist to her hand and squeezed it. She slowly lifted her face to meet his consoling gaze. Her heartbeat raced in her chest. "I'm so sorry. Ashley's dead."

Bridget's hands sought the release of the too-tight seat belt. "This had nothing to do with the clinic. Did it?" *Did it?* This was a horrible, unrelated tragedy. Ashley had been jogging alone on a bike path. That's what it was. Her death was unrelated to the apartment fire, to the near miss in the crosswalk. It had to be.

"My business card was crammed down her throat."

Bridget bent over and covered her face with her hands. "This is all my fault."

She felt Zach's warm hand on her arm. "This is not your fault," he whispered. "Please stay here, for your safety."

She pulled her hands away from her face and swiped at a tear. "I can't. I'm not welcomed."

"Your parents must understand." He tipped his head to look out the passenger window. Cornfields waved in the wind.

She shook her head. "*You* don't understand." She sniffed. *Hold it together.*

"I have to keep you safe until they find the parties responsible." His phone dinged, and he quickly checked it. If the text had anything to do with her or Ashley or Dr. Ryan, he didn't say.

Every fiber of her body vibrated with the nightmare she found herself in. "My father won't let me stay. Perhaps if you can convince him?" Bridget knew she was taking the coward's way out. She also knew that her father could never be swayed from his convictions, especially by an outsider.

SIX

Zach followed Bridget, a step behind, as she readjusted the bonnet on her head after ripping it off in frustration moments ago. She frantically tucked fine strands of hair under the white material, as if donning armor to approach her father. Her upswept hair exposed her delicate neck. She carefully navigated the rutted driveway. There was much he wanted to ask her about growing up in an Amish community, but it would have to wait. He was about to get a crash course in what it would take to convince a stern Amish father to allow his prodigal daughter to return—albeit temporarily. Zach'd appeal to the man's sense of paternal love. That should be universal. His daughter's life was in danger.

Unfortunately, not all parents were created equal. His own mother came to mind, and he quickly dismissed the thought. This case was challenging his finely honed skills of compartmentalization.

"He's never going to go for this," Bridget muttered when they reached the steps to the front porch. "I was foolish to come back. Or maybe I was foolish to report what I saw at the clinic."

Before Zach had a chance to reassure her, a man he suspected was her father opened the front door and stepped out onto the porch. He crossed his arms over his chest and arranged his face in a stern expression. Bridget came by her conclusions that this was going to be a hard sell honestly. Her mother joined them. Her body language softened, but the subtle tip of her head suggested she'd defer to her husband.

"You came back," her father said without much emotion.

"*Yah*. This is…" Bridget seemed to be debating how to introduce Zach. Since she had hoped to keep him away from her parents, they had never discussed this. Perhaps they'd respond to the bold truth.

"Sir, ma'am—" He offered his hand, and when neither made an effort to accept it, he dropped it. "I'm Agent Zach Bryant."

"This is my mother, Mae, and my father, Amos," Bridget said.

"Your daughter—"

"What did you do?" Her father glared at her.

"Sir, your daughter has been very brave."

"Too brave, if you ask me." Amos shifted his crossed arms under his long beard.

Next to Zach, Bridget drew in a shaky breath. Her mother gently touched her husband's arm. Her father tipped his straw hat slightly, suggesting Zach should go on.

"Bridget needs a place to stay," Zach said, "for a short time."

"We're not a hotel." Amos's lips twitched. "What's going on, and is there a reason my daughter's not speaking for herself?" He adjusted his stance and slipped his thumbs under his suspenders. He was definitely a man who ruled his home. Zach supposed there was nothing wrong with having a strong male role model, as long as he was a benevolent leader.

"*Dat.*" Bridget spoke up. "A friend of mine was killed,

and I'm afraid the same people are going to hurt me." Her voice held a confidence that surprised Zach.

"Oh dear." Her mother pressed a hand to her chest. *"Umkumme...?" Killed*, she muttered.

"You have brought this on yourself by going into the outside world. You didn't believe me when I told you about the evil in the *Englisch* world." Her father shook his head in disgust.

Zach bit back his strong impulse to defend Bridget and gave her room to do it herself. He couldn't believe her father was willing to make a judgment without knowing the details.

"Can I stay or not?" Bridget spit out. "I promise I won't be here long."

A muscle ticked in her father's jaw. He obviously wasn't used to his daughter speaking to him like this.

"Please." Bridget softened her tone, seemingly resigned that she'd have to mend fences if she wanted to stay in Hickory Lane. "I'm tired and I'm scared."

Her father's posture relaxed, seemingly receptive to his daughter's apology. "Why was your friend killed and why are they after you?"

Zach gently touched Bridget's hand. "It would be better if we didn't discuss that."

"You're asking to stay in my home," her father said, his voice even.

"Yah, Dat. I never told anyone I was Amish. No one would ever find me here." Bridget smiled tightly. "I would never knowingly put my family in danger."

His nostrils flared, and it seemed to take considerable restraint for him not to speak his mind.

"Amos, we can find it in our hearts to let our daughter come home," her mother said, a pleading quality to her voice.

Amos tipped his head slightly and turned on his heel and strode down the porch steps toward the barn. Her mother turned to them. "You are welcome to come home, Bridget."

"What about *Dat*?" Across the yard, Amos yanked open the barn door and then disappeared inside.

"In his own way, he has agreed. Don't push him," her mother warned. "Your friend cannot stay here, though. That would get the neighbors talking." Her warm gaze met Zach's. "The Amish like to stay separate. That includes from those in law enforcement."

He nodded. "I understand." Truth be told, he understood nothing about the Amish. "I'll check in at the hotel in town."

"Why do you need to stay in town? No one knows I'm here," Bridget said. "Why can't you go back to Buffalo and let me know when it's safe to return home?"

"You are home," her mother whispered, and for the first time Zach could see how Bridget's coming here was going to take an emotional toll on her entire family.

How did he explain that he couldn't leave her unprotected? He refused to make another mistake that cost an innocent person their life, never mind that he was supposed to be on leave from the DEA. For now, that made it easier because he could do whatever he thought necessary without clearing it with his supervisor. "I'll stay close for now. Maybe that will change," he said to appease her.

Bridget seemed to regard him with a sense of apprehension.

"I'll be right in town. Minutes away." Then he turned to her mother. "Nice to meet you, Mrs. Miller," Zach said before descending the porch steps. He decided against giving Bridget last-minute instructions to keep a low profile. She was a smart woman, and he didn't want to cause more concern for her sweet mother, who seemed to be basking in the glow of her long-lost daughter's return. Zach's goal was to keep Bridget safe, not meddle in family dynamics that were far more complicated than his pay grade, especially because he was technically off duty.

Bridget stood on the porch of her childhood home and watched Zach pull away in his truck. A wave of unease pressed into her heart. It was hard to imagine that twenty-four hours ago she was taking blood pressure and weights of patients before they saw the doctor, trying to act like everything was okay. Had Dr. Ryan suspected anything? Not possible. He had been his usual friendly self.

A soft breeze blew a stray strand of hair across her face. With the hook of her finger, she tugged it away and turned to take in the farm. Her mother and sister had disappeared into the house. Inside the barn across the way, her father was probably taking his aggression out on his chores. She imagined her brothers were in the barn doing their chores, too, otherwise they would have come to greet her.

Bridget lowered herself onto the top step and smoothed her skirt. Her brothers. They had been little guys when she left. Soon they'd be about to embark on their own adventures. Bending forward, she hugged her thighs. She had really missed her family. She had kept homesickness at bay by not letting herself think about what she was missing. Now that she was back here, she could no longer deny her sense of loss.

When she had left under the cloak of darkness all those years ago, she feared the only time she'd ever return would be to help bury her parents. She was grateful to have this time with her parents while still on this side of heaven. Sadly, her return wouldn't lead to some grand reconciliation, not unless she got down on bended knee, then received baptism and married.

There would be no happily-ever-after for her here among the Amish.

Bridget closed her eyes and inhaled. Sweet grass. A hint of manure. Dried cornstalks. *Familiar.* She blinked away the threatening tears. She couldn't put this homecoming—however temporary—off any longer. She rose to her feet and crossed the porch to the screen door, the same one she had carefully closed so her parents wouldn't hear her leave in the middle of the night.

She stepped inside, this time not caring if the door clacked in its frame behind her. She followed the smell of her mother's fresh-baked bread. "Hi, *Mem.*" Her mother was stirring something on the stove.

Her mother set the wooden spoon on the ceramic rest and turned around. A small smile that spoke volumes curved her lips. "You're just in time to help with preparations for tomorrow."

Bridget scrunched up her nose, momentarily confused. "You're hosting Sunday service tomorrow?" What unfortunate timing.

"*Yah*, and many hands make light work."

Renewed dread pooled in her gut. She'd have to face the entire community. Maybe she could hide in her bedroom.

"Could you help your sister cut the celery?" her mother asked.

"Um…sure." Bridget locked gazes with Liddie who seemed to be enjoying herself.

Her mother wiped her hands on her apron. "The celery has already been rinsed."

Bridget grabbed a knife and another cutting board and began chopping. The activity, here with her mother and sister, brought her back to a life she'd thought she had abandoned forever. Liddie playfully nudged her with her elbow, and Bridget rolled her eyes.

A moment later there was a commotion at the side door leading into the mudroom adjacent to the kitchen. Two young men she barely recognized stood there watching her with wide eyes. "*Dat* said you were home. I had to see for myself," Elijah said, his voice cracking. He was no longer a little boy.

The youngest brother was more reserved. Caleb had been so much younger when Bridget left Hickory Lane.

"It's really me." Bridget set the knife down. "My, how you boys have grown." She gestured with her chin toward Elijah. "The girls must be swarming around you at Sunday singings."

"The only thing that's swarming around him are the flies," Caleb deadpanned, scrunching up his nose.

"Now, that's not nice," their mother scolded. "Now go clean up for lunch. Your sister will make you sandwiches."

Without missing a beat, Bridget made her brothers sandwiches and set them on plates on the table. The boys disappeared and returned after washing their hands. They slipped into their chairs and scarfed down their food. When she was growing up here, they were never allowed to eat until their father had sat down at the head of the table. She wondered what else had changed since she left.

She went back to help her mom make food preparations for tomorrow. A rustling sounded at the back door, and Bridget found herself tightening her grip around the knife. She set it down and waited for the inevitability of the confrontation with her dad.

Suddenly she felt sixteen again the morning after she had missed her Sunday-night curfew. Moses Lapp, a boy who liked her, had refused to take her home, instead insisting they hang out with a few other young couples. Bridget didn't feel comfortable among her Amish peers. They were pairing up with the intention of settling down. Her good friend Katy came to mind. Bridget had no doubt she was married and wondered how many kids she had by now.

She released a slow breath. She wasn't that same girl.

Her father sat down at his place at the table without saying a word. The air hung thick with tension.

"Bridget, your father would like a sandwich," her mother said.

"She should not be serving me food." Her father pushed back from the table and stilled, his arms crossed over his suspenders like a petulant child.

Her mother held out her hand, encouraging him to relax. "I'll get it. I'm sorry. I got distracted with everything going on," Mae said apologetically.

"We don't need any more distractions around here," her father said, placing his hands flat on the table, not looking in Bridget's direction. "We have a lot of preparation to do for tomorrow. We need a little less horseplay from Elijah and Caleb, or we could have had the barn swept out already. And don't forget Levi should be here with the benches after lunch."

"We'll get it all done," her mother said reassuringly. "We always do." Each family in the district took turns hosting Sunday service every other week. Due to the size of the district, each family only had to host it once every year—or at least, that's how it had always been.

"Too many distractions," her father muttered again.

A knot twisted in Bridget's heart. Since she had secreted away, she had only imagined the stress she had created by leaving. She had imagined that her family had been going on with their lives just as before, but without her. Seeing them now made her sadder. Leaving had affected everyone. Why had she been so selfish? Because she wanted to become a nurse.

Bridget found herself mute in the presence of her father. She had always been afraid of him. He ruled with an iron fist. She dried her hands on her apron, then stepped out on the back porch, leaving only the screen door between them. The community would gather tomorrow at her childhood home, and she would be forced to stay separate. It would only cause problems for her parents if they didn't make an example of her.

Maybe she'd get to hide out in her bedroom after all.

"Here's your lunch." Bridget could hear her mother's soothing voice through the screen door. Forever the peacemaker.

"Mae, she will remain separate. She cannot dine with us. She cannot worship with us. We cannot condone her actions," her father instructed her mother. "Until she repents and goes down on bended knee in front of the bishop, she must be under the *Bann*."

Anger began to replace the emptiness in Bridget's heart. Her father couldn't even use her name. She grabbed the handle on the screen door and yanked it open. The door bounced off the wood siding, then swung back and slammed shut in its frame. She stormed into the kitchen. "*Dat*, I have no plans to stay longer than I have to."

Her father's dark eyes flared wide, obviously surprised by her outburst. She had never confronted him. Until now. "Perhaps you should leave now, then. Since you're too ashamed to tell anyone that you come from an Amish home."

"Why would I tell anyone? They'd only think I was a freak." Bridget's pulse roared in her ears. Bile tickled the back of her throat. Exploding at her father would serve no purpose other than to release the anger and fear she had been bottling up since Zach told her Ashley was dead.

Liddie spun around from where she worked at the counter. Her face was blotchy, and she seemed on the verge of tears. "You have to let her stay."

"Apparently, I don't have much control over what she does. She has ears but doesn't listen." Her father narrowed his gaze at her. "*She*—" her father emphasized the word, making Bridget wonder if he'd ever use her name "—made her decision when she crept out of here in the middle of the night. She didn't have the decency to say goodbye to your mother."

"Bridget's in danger," Liddie said, alarm in her voice.

"It's okay, Liddie." Bridget willed her sister to stop talking.

"She has nowhere else to go. Someone smashed the window in her apartment, and it went up in flames. If Bridget had been in her bedroom, she might have been really hurt. Agent Bryant already told you her coworker was murdered."

"Murdered," Caleb said, his tone a mix between being horrified and intrigued.

"Liddie," Bridget warned her sister again, "please."

Their father held up his hand. "We should have never allowed you to go to Buffalo, Liddie. It only exposed you to the evils of the outside world. It was a mistake. And now you have brought your drama here."

A groundswell of anger and disbelief pressed on Bridget's lungs. Hearing how easily her father dismissed recent events was too much.

"*Dat*, I had no intention of sharing the details of my life in Buffalo." She lifted her chin and met her father's dark eyes. *Why can't you love me for who I am?* "I'll get out of your way."

"No!" Liddie yelled. She clasped her hands together and pressed them to her chest. "No one is listening. We have to make sure Bridget is safe. She can't leave."

Mem repeatedly dried her hands on the dish towel. Their father took a bite of his sandwich, then swallowed. He dabbed at his lips. A crumb settled in his unkempt beard. The silence filled the room with heavy expectation. "*She* will eat separate from us. *She* will have chores. If and only if she is ready to ask for forgiveness and be baptized, she can fully join this family. We will not discuss the outside world."

Apparently, Bridget had been invited to stay. On *Dat*'s terms. On Amish terms.

She wouldn't be staying for a minute longer than she had to.

SEVEN

Later that night, Zach found himself driving along the country roads and staring up at the spectacular display of stars visible in the dark night sky. He had been unable to sleep due to the commotion of a few teenagers who had congregated on bicycles in the motel parking lot. Their laughter and loud voices traveled through the thin walls. He could have easily sent them on their way, but his objective was to be low-key, not announce his presence by annoying a handful of bored locals who weren't really bothering anyone except him.

Zach navigated the roads to the Miller farm. He parked on the side of the road. Back at the motel, he had searched "Amish" on the internet. After scrolling past several hits on reality shows—which he took a leap and assumed weren't actually "reality"—he clicked on a few sites that discussed the basic tenets of the Amish. Prior to his dive down the rabbit hole, he hadn't known much about the Amish other than the fact that they didn't drive cars or use electricity. Their lifestyle was fascinating. From his cursory search, he now had a sense of why Bridget was reluctant to return. The Amish didn't take kindly to those who left and often shunned those who did, unless they asked for forgiveness.

Zach pushed open the truck's door, and the sound of

crickets filled the night air, louder than he had ever heard. The blackness swallowed him. The weight of his gun on his hip was reassuring. It took a moment for his eyes to adjust. He looked up and immediately spotted the Little Dipper, sadly the only constellation he could name. It reminded him of the time his parents had taken him and his sister to the beach when they were kids. He had never experienced the night sky without light pollution before. Back when life was still innocent. Back when he and his sister were best buddies and their biggest concern was keeping sand out of their eyes and reapplying sunscreen.

Back before his mother had back surgery and started taking prescription drugs. Back before his father bailed because he was unable or unwilling to manage a family spiraling out of control.

Zach's thoughts came fast and frantic, like cracks in thinning ice, promising to plunge him into icy-cold water, drowning him. A break from work was the worst thing for him. He needed to keep busy to outrun his thoughts. To make meaning of all the tragedy he had experienced.

He tilted his head from side to side to ease the kinks in his neck. He scanned the Miller farm while he strolled toward the house. He strained his ears for anything out of the ordinary. He chuckled to himself. What was out of the ordinary on an Amish farm? There were no vehicles parked anywhere nearby, so unless the bad guys discovered her location and stomped through the woods or across the fields, Bridget should be safe.

Zach made a sweep of the grounds. Other than the house and barn, there was one other outbuilding. Bridget had mentioned that her grandfather lived there. The stillness was so complete, the kind that could only be achieved in the country on a property where they didn't use electricity. There wasn't even the hum of a generator competing with the sounds of nature. He'd go back to his motel room and wait for morning.

There was nothing for him to do here.

Any leads would be in Buffalo. Zach had made a few calls, and a coworker in the DEA office was doing some digging. Standing on the sidelines made him itchy. His supervisor claimed that what he did on his leave was his business, but he doubted she'd go for this. He hoped she wouldn't extend his leave if he pushed his involvement here too far. Or maybe she'd realize making him take a break was pointless. It wouldn't change what happened. He was good at his job. He thrived on his undercover work. He had a knack for getting on the inside, gaining the trust of strangers who didn't generally trust people. The key was to cut off the head of an organization and not focus solely on easy arrests, like the street-level dealers. Dealers were easily replaceable. The traffickers higher up the chain of command needed to be the focal point.

And here he was on the far, far sidelines, sidestepping horse manure on an Amish farm. He laughed to himself at the absurdity of it, then suddenly froze when the distinct scent of sweet tobacco reached him. He tilted his head, and this time he heard shoes shuffling on gravel. He sank back closer to one of the buildings and watched a dark figure emerge from around the side of the structure. The person moved slowly, taking deliberate steps. Before Zach had a chance to say anything, a raspy voice said, "Are you the man who brought my granddaughter home?"

Zach stepped away from the building. Under the stars, light glistened in the elderly gentleman's eyes. His hair was mussed, and a straggly beard extended down his chest. "Yes, I'm Special Agent Zach Bryant with the DEA."

"DEA?" the elderly man asked.

"Drug Enforcement Administration."

The man harrumphed. "I don't know anything about that. All I know is that you made my daughter Mae happy by bringing Bridget home."

"I wish it could have been under better circumstances."

"*Yah*, well, I suppose if things had been better, she wouldn't have come home."

"I didn't expect to run into anyone in the middle of the night. Is everything okay?" Zach looked around, not able see much in the heavy shadows. He kept his phone and its flashlight app in his pocket, because he didn't want to be rude.

"I guess I could ask you the same. Is everything okay?" The elderly man ran his hand down his beard in slow, deliberate sweeps.

"Yes, everything seems to be quiet tonight."

"That's why we live here." He seemed to regard his surroundings. "Nice and quiet. Separate from the outside world."

"I can see the appeal," Zach said. "Some local kids decided to throw an impromptu party in the parking lot of the motel. Made it a little hard to sleep."

"Hmm." The elderly man seemed to consider that. "Well, I'm old. Don't sleep much anyway. I enjoy getting out at night." He looked up at the stars. "Soon the evenings will grow chilly." He turned his attention on Zach. "If you think it's quiet now, come out here when the ground's covered with snow. *Friedlich.*"

Zach narrowed his gaze and after a beat, the other man said, *"Peaceful."*

Zach had taken two years of German in high school and he had learned in his internet search that Pennsylvania Dutch was a derivation of German, not that he was going to respond in kind.

"I'll have to take your word on that. I'm not much for

the cold," Zach said, for lack of anything else to say. It seemed people of all walks loved to talk weather.

The elderly man tipped his head again. "*Mei enkelin* is in danger? My granddaughter was never content here."

Zach ran a hand over the itchy stubble on his jaw, deciding to be straight with this man, if not overly generous with the specifics. "Yes, she was witness to something at work, and she was very brave to come forward. Now it seems she made some people unhappy."

"Unhappy?" Bridget's grandfather planted his cane and took another step. "*Unhappy* seems to be an understatement. Her friend was found dead. And you work for the DEA. Do I understand correctly?"

Zach's lips twitched at the elderly man's candor. "You didn't misunderstand, sir, I'm sorry to say."

The elderly man lifted his cane a fraction. "My name's Jeremiah. Might as well get used to calling me that if you're going to be hanging around."

"My name's Zach."

"Nice to meet you, Zach. I trust you'll keep Bridget safe."

"I'll do my best, sir." Zach wasn't sure how long he was going to be hanging around. Bridget should be safe here where no one would think to look for her.

"Jeremiah," Bridget's grandfather repeated.

"Yes, s— Jeremiah. I understand you live on the property. In this separate house?"

"*Yah*, right here. It's nice that the Amish take care of their old folk."

"I imagine it is." When the silence stretched out a beat too long, Zach said, "Well, I better head back to the motel for some shut-eye." He turned toward the road.

"You'll need rest for tomorrow. Lots of work to be done." Jeremiah took a few limping steps toward the small structure from which he had emerged, then he paused. "I have an extra cot. Stay here."

Zach lifted his head. "I'm fine at the motel."

Jeremiah shrugged. "No youths rabble-rousing around here. Grab some shut-eye. We could use a few more strong hands to make sure the benches are arranged in the barn."

"The benches?"

"*Yah*, they need to be set up in the barn. The entire community will arrive early for the nine o'clock worship service."

The aroma of coffee woke Zach from a sound sleep. He rolled over on the narrow cot, and a metal bar that had been jabbing into his back now pressed into his hip. Despite the thin mattress, he had fallen asleep almost as soon as Jeremiah pointed to the folded-up cot at the far wall of an oversize pantry. All he had to do was pop it open and make it up. With the window open a crack, he fell asleep to the sound of nature and not teenage boys goofing off.

Grunting, he pushed to a seated position and wiped the sleep out of his eyes. The first hint of dawn had softened the darkness outside the small window. He reached over and checked the time on his smartphone. *Ugh*, it was early. He strained to listen, surprised he couldn't hear a rooster crowing. Instead, he heard the shuffling around of Jeremiah outside the pantry where they had set up Zach's cot, his host's idea of privacy.

Zach slipped on his pants and T-shirt and ran a hand over his hair. He could zip back to the motel, shower and get back in time to help with whatever chores Jeremiah had lined up for him. He didn't mind staying busy. He'd also have to talk to Bridget about the long-term plan. Yesterday had been about getting Bridget to safety. Today was making sure she didn't run back to Buffalo too soon.

He stuffed his feet into his shoes and stepped out into the kitchen with his laces still untied. Jeremiah sat at the small kitchen table drinking coffee and reading a newspaper.

"Guder mariye."

Half of Zach's mouth curved into a smile. "Um...good morning." He really should have paid more attention in German class.

"How did you sleep?" the elderly gentleman asked before taking another sip from his mug. "There's a pot of coffee on the stove. *Schnell! Schnell!*" The old man frowned. "Hurry. We have a lot to do."

"I'm going to run back to the motel and clean up. I'll grab coffee later."

Jeremiah set down his mug. "No time for that. Last-minute chores still need to be done. You need to change." He lifted his cane that leaned against the table and pointed. "I set some clothes on the bench there."

Zach followed the man's cane to a neat pile of men's clothing. *Amish clothes.* "I have fresh clothes at the motel. It won't take me long."

Jeremiah lifted a bushy gray eyebrow. "No need. Get dressed, move your truck into the *Englisch* neighbor's driveway about a half mile down the road. We have a good relationship with our neighbors. Then get back here to help with the preparations. If you plan on protecting my granddaughter, you need to fit in."

Zach scooped up the clothes and held them to his chest, suddenly feeling compelled to follow the orders of his host.

"The clothes should fit. I used to be a little taller before my back issues." Jeremiah smoothed his hand over the newspaper spread in front of him. "If they need any tailoring, I'm sure Bridget can handle that for you."

Zach smothered the smile pulling at his lips. He didn't

know Bridget well, but he suspected asking her to tailor his clothes wasn't going to ingratiate him to her.

"I'll get dressed." Zach had spent a large portion of his young career with the DEA working undercover to get some of the most dangerous criminals, pretending to be someone he wasn't to get information he needed. He'd have to regard this as more of the same. Sort of.

He closed the door in the pantry and picked up the pair of trousers with a hook and eye closure. No zipper. Interesting. He held them to his waist. They might fit. He tossed off his T-shirt and put on the dark blue shirt.

"I have a pair of suspenders out here for you."

Zach dragged his thumb around the waistband of his pants. "I think I might need that." He smoothed his hands down his shirt, wishing he had a full-length mirror. Less than forty-eight hours ago, he had had an appointment to meet Bridget and Ashley for a tip related to potential health-care fraud, and now he was on an Amish farm about to see if he looked good in plain clothing.

A rapping sounded at the door. "You best get moving. Your truck parked out front is going to raise a lot of questions."

"I'm on it." Zach yanked open the door. "I'll move it right now."

Jeremiah extended his hand with a pair of suspenders.

Zach took them and fastened them to his pants. He rolled back on his heels and patted his midsection. "How do I look?" He supposed his black sneakers would pass.

Jeremiah raised a bushy eyebrow and nodded. "It'll do. It'll have to."

Zach hooked his thumbs under his suspenders then let them snap. "Ouch."

Jeremiah shook his head with a hint of amusement.

"You can admire yourself later." He reached over and snagged a straw hat off a hook. "You'll need this, too."

Zach stuffed it on his head and hustled out the door and down the dirt driveway. The country air smelled sweet. Fresh.

He had officially entered another world.

Bridget rose before the rest of her family and mixed some instant coffee with hot water from the stove, since she was too lazy to mess with the French press. She missed the coffee maker at home, a rare splurge for her. Grabbing the mug of black coffee, she slipped outside and settled into one of the rockers on the back porch. She missed the stillness of the country, but she hadn't missed how conflicted she had been while growing up here. She had always known there was more in the world but feared that going after more would condemn her spiritually.

Settling back into the rocker, she took another sip of coffee. Maybe during her short stay she could make peace—however fragile—with her family. Escaping during the middle of the night had made her departure more painful.

With her bare foot, she rocked slowly. It was such a soothing motion. As a kid, she used to sit here with a book until her *dat* scolded her and told her to get back to her chores. The memory made her smile. *Englisch* parents would take pride in their children reading instead of being hunched over smartphones or tablets. She had watched them, fascinated, in the waiting room of the clinic, almost oblivious to anything going on around them.

The clinic.

Dr. Ryan.

Ashley. Poor, poor Ashley.

Icy dread pooled in her stomach. Had Ashley's parents been notified? Did her siblings know? Bridget had worked long days with Ashley, yet she didn't know a ton about her family life. Now she never would. Tears pricked the backs of her eyes.

What have I done? If I had never told her about what I saw...

Maybe she'd check her cell phone for any news later. It was tucked away in her bedroom wardrobe, and digging it out would wake Liddie.

Drawing in the rich aroma of the coffee, she kept up the rocking motion, trying to root herself in the moment. *Let go and let God.* It wasn't exactly a Bible verse, but she had clung to the mantra after she heard it in the home of the woman who took her in when she first left Hickory Lane. She stared out over the land that hadn't changed, other than through the seasons, since she had left. The familiarity of that was soothing. The first streaks of pink and purple stretched across the sky. She smiled to herself. When was the last time she sat and studied the sky? She had been so busy with work and school.

Soon, her brothers would be up, feeding the animals and mucking out the stalls. Bridget hadn't missed that one bit.

Out of the corner of her eye, she noticed something moving out in the field. She turned her attention toward it, fully expecting a deer. Or maybe the neighbor's cow had broken through the fence again. She squinted and tucked in her chin. It was a person.

Panic sliced through the early morning tranquility. She slid forward on the rocker, and the chair dipped low. Her feet melded to the wooden planks. Her heart raced, and her fight-or-flight response kicked in. She planted her hand on the edge of the chair and stood, her knees wobbly under her.

Had *they* found her?

She spun around, her long skirt swooshing around her

ankles, and reached for the door handle, fearing that she had brought danger to her family's doorstep. The latch caught. She glanced over her shoulder and nearly collapsed against the back door with utter and complete relief.

"You scared me," Bridget said, wiping her sweaty palms on the folds of her dress. "What are you doing?" She stepped off the porch, the damp earth cool on her toes, and gave DEA Special Agent Zach Bryant a once-over. "How? Why? Who gave you those clothes?" The first hint of amusement sparked in Bridget's chest, a welcomed reprieve from the sadness and uncertainty that had kept her tossing and turning last night.

"You want the long or the short version?" Zach tugged on his suspenders and smiled. She wasn't sure if it was the relief that she was safe or the early morning lighting that made him seem vulnerable. Human. Less law enforcement–like. Maybe it was because the plain clothing had softened his hard edges.

"Want coffee? I've got time for the long version." She turned to go in.

"No, wait. Sit." Zach stepped up onto the porch and held out his hand to one of the rockers. She sat, and Zach sat next to her. "I had to move my truck. Your grandfather told me to park it at the neighbor's. Walking across the field seemed like the quickest route back."

"Yeah, to giving me a heart attack."

"Sorry, I didn't realize you'd see me." He kept his tone hushed, almost reverent.

"Why are you here already?" She furrowed her brow. "And dressed in those clothes? What did I miss? Did something happen?" Her tendency to pepper someone with questions when she was nervous was in full force.

"Nothing new to report, so no worries there." He slid back in the rocker and ran his strong hands up and down the smooth arms of the chair. "I couldn't sleep, so I drove over last night to make sure the farm was secure, and I ran into your grandfather."

Bridget smiled. "No further explanation needed." Her grandfather exuded quiet authority. *Mem* claimed he was a force to be reckoned with when he was a younger man, but he had allowed the next generation to take up the mantle after his wife died and he settled into the *dawdy haus*.

Zach seemed to study her for a moment. "Should I be worried about your grandfather?" He offered her a bemused smile.

"No, of all my family, I always felt like he was the one who understood me. I mean, I could never confide in him regarding my plans to leave. I didn't want to do that to him. He sensed I wanted more, though." She set her empty coffee mug down on the porch floor and leaned back in the chair and resumed rocking. "I felt his quiet support."

"Do you miss living here?"

"I've missed my family. Living here is a world away. A completely different culture. I could never be a nurse here."

"I don't mean to pry with all my questions. The Amish way of life is fascinating."

"A lot of people feel the same way. That's why there are so many tourists." She was unable to hide the disdain in her voice. Most tourists were respectful, but she had had enough bad run-ins to make her weary.

"I was thinking of Ashley this morning," Bridget said, needing to change the subject. "Did someone let her family know?"

"Yes, her family was notified." There was a faraway quality to his voice.

"Her poor family." She let out a shaky breath. "This is all my fault." She stilled and shifted in her seat to face Zach.

He surprised her by reaching out and covering her hand on the arm of the chair. "This is *not* your fault. You hear me?"

A lump in her throat kept her from doing more than nodding. She pulled her hand out from under his. "How long do you think I'll have to stay here?"

Zach ran a hand over his scratchy jaw, debating. She had gotten good at reading people; she had spent a lifetime reading her father's moods and then used that skill to read her patients.

"I don't know. My office has people on it. I'm thinking I could expedite the process if I returned to Buffalo." She sensed he wasn't telling her something.

Bridget's heart sank. She wasn't sure why. It wasn't like she didn't feel safe here. Not without him. This was ridiculous. She had just met him. Maybe it was because he represented security. Or a link to her new life. If he left, would that somehow leave her unanchored back in a life that she never wanted?

Apparently sensing her concern, he said, "We have to locate Dr. Ryan. He needs to answer our questions. Then we'll know exactly what we're dealing with."

"What about the clinic?" She had been so worried about her situation, she had neglected to consider the community that relied on the clinic. "Many people have nowhere else to go." What had she done? A groundswell of self-doubt threatened to overwhelm her.

"My office is searching the clinic today. Depending on what they find, the clinic could be shut down indefinitely. In past cases like this, the clinic eventually reopens under a new director." He made a smacking sound with his lips. "I won't lie—it may take time."

"You mentioned you were on leave from your job," she said, leaving her comment open-ended, hoping he'd explain.

"Let me worry about that."

"Okay."

"You did the right thing," he said, realizing Ashley's death weighted heavily on her.

"Ashley wouldn't think so."

"Ashley had a mind of her own. You didn't coerce her into doing anything."

"I'm not so sure." Bridget bit her lower lip.

"I am. She was best friends with my sister, Leann." There was a strange quality to his voice. "Ashley had a strong personality. No way you talked her into anything she already wasn't on board with."

"Your sister must be devastated."

"My sister's dead."

"Oh, I'm sorry." Tingles raced across her scalp.

"It was a long time ago." He spoke softly and stared straight ahead over the field. "She overdosed. Ashley was with her."

A band of sympathy squeezed all the air from her lungs. "I'm truly sorry. I had no idea." Why hadn't Ashley shared that piece of information? No doubt, it had been too painful for everyone.

Zach tapped his index finger on the arm of the rocker. "Leann's tragic death shaped the course of my life." He seemed lost in thought, yet eager to tell his sister's story. "I was serving overseas at the time. I hadn't realized how bad her drug use had gotten."

Had Ashley been involved with drugs, too? Bridget didn't want to ask. Tarnishing her friend's memory seemed disrespectful in light of her death.

The weight of guilt slumped his shoulders. No reassurances from her would lift the burden. She understood guilt. She was wallowing in the deep end of it right now. "Is that why you're a DEA agent?"

His face transformed into something painfully handsome when he smiled sadly at her. "Yes. Sometimes I wonder why. It feels futile. The drug problem in this country is enormous. In the case of your clinic, it'll most likely be shut down once they uncover the problem, a few arrests will be made, but the traffickers will find another healthcare provider looking to make some quick cash. Money they're willing to risk their lives for."

Hearing him talk like this wasn't very reassuring. "You're doing what you can."

"It never seems like enough. We need to find a way to end this horrible epidemic before more people die."

Despite his determination, they both knew more people would die.

EIGHT

Bridget watched in awe as Zach joined right in with preparations for Sunday service. She helped with last-minute food prep, and if her participation wasn't warranted due to the *Bann*, no one said anything. She suspected her father would remind her of her place before the first guest arrived. Appearances were everything.

Bridget set the loaf of bread on the table and turned to wipe the crumbs from the counter. From the window over the sink, she watched the guests climb out of their buggies and greet her mother. Her brothers were charged with unhitching the horses and taking them to the fenced-in field. While the female guests would stop into the house with their covered dishes, the men would gather outside until they were called in for the service.

As the first group of women approached the house, a wave of unease warmed Bridget's skin. She plucked at her white cape covering her dress. She had forgotten how warm it could get with fabric down to her ankles in this heat. Her mother gestured to the house with a bright smile. The Amish neighbors turned their gazes toward the house—toward her?—with wide eyes and polite smiles. Bridget ducked away from the window. Perhaps her mother was eager to let everyone know that her daughter was home. Perhaps the circumstances didn't matter. She *was* home. Her mother had hope. The impulse to run upstairs and hide was strong. But Bridget didn't want to embarrass her mother by disappearing upstairs.

A thudding sound snapped Bridget's attention toward the stairs. Liddie appeared flushed, excited, as if she were hiding a secret.

"Where have you been? I thought you'd be down here helping already," Bridget said, regretting her harsh tone that had nothing to do with Liddie's absence.

Her little sister smiled. "I was helping earlier…" she lowered her voice to a whisper "…I had to make a call."

"You didn't get rid of your phone?" Bridget was careful to keep her voice low.

Liddie shrugged, a mischievous smile splitting her face. "Don't tell."

"I wouldn't dare." Bridget checked out the window. The women were still chatting. "Who were you talking to?"

"I'll tell you later." Liddie tucked a wayward strand of hair under her bonnet. Her attention also shifted toward the window. "Do you think I could go back to Buffalo with you?"

"What? Why?"

Liddie adjusted her cape over her dress. "No, don't worry. I'm not going to leave Hickory Lane. I'd like to visit again. That's all." Her tone held a forced casualness.

"Why?" Bridget studied her sister's face. Liddie wouldn't meet her eyes, a tell that her sister wasn't being completely honest.

"I made a friend."

"The person you were talking to on the phone."

Liddie hitched a shoulder and her eyes shone brightly.

Bridget narrowed her eyes slightly. Her questions would have to wait for another time. "*Mem* and *Dat* would never allow it. Besides, I have no idea where I'm going to be living." She shook her head tightly, too stressed to deal with her sister's request. "No. It's not going to happen."

Liddie rolled her eyes. "I could always do what you did and leave in the middle of the night."

Bridget felt like she had been sucker punched. "You said you weren't going to leave Hickory Lane." The excited chatter of the women grew closer to the screen door. "Can we talk about this later?"

"Sure," Liddie said, making a final adjustment to her bonnet. "Zach looks handsome in plain clothes." Her sister's eyes flashed mischievously. "Do you suppose he's hiding his gun somewhere under there?"

"Hush," Bridget said, shoving a pitcher of water at her sister. "Put this on the table. The older folk should stay hydrated." Memories of sitting in a sweltering barn or airless home on a backless bench floated to mind. If staying separate meant she couldn't go to service today, she'd take it.

"Listen to the nurse," Liddie teased, apparently in an especially good mood. Then she waved her hand in dismissal. "It's not like we haven't seen someone pass out at a service before."

"I'm trying to prevent that."

Before Liddie had a chance to argue, their mother came bustling in with a few women. Each placed a covered dish on the table to stay safe from bugs until after the service, when everything would be carried outside for the communal meal.

Bridget found herself averting her gaze while she tidied up from the preparations.

"Hello, Bridget."

She looked up to find Mrs. Yoder standing in front of her, a strained smile on her face. "You've come home?" Her somber tone reflected her obvious skepticism.

Bridget felt her mother's gaze on her. They hadn't discussed what she should tell the neighbors, perhaps assuming Bridget would stay safely tucked away. Obviously, they hadn't thought this through.

"We're happy to have her home," Bridget's mother answered for her. "She's been a big help in getting everything ready today."

"Oh…" Mrs. Yoder seemed at a loss for words.

"How is Katy?" Bridget quickly asked about Mrs. Yoder's oldest daughter, who had been one of Bridget's best friends growing up. Through Liddie, Bridget learned that the bishop had come down especially hard on Katy after Bridget jumped the fence. Some people suspected she knew. That Katy had helped her friend leave. Of course, none of that was true. Bridget had left without telling a soul.

Mrs. Yoder straightened her back and smiled. "My Katy is happily married and keeping a wonderful home." She got a faraway look in her eyes. "She has two little ones." No doubt, Mrs. Yoder was relieved her daughter hadn't been tainted by her childhood friend who had broken the rules of the *Ordnung*.

"I'm happy for her. Please tell her I said hello." Then in a burst of nostalgia, she added, "I've missed her."

Mrs. Yoder's lip twitched, and she seemed to be holding something back.

"If you'll excuse me, I have a few more things to do before the service." Bridget tipped her head and brushed past the women. She whispered to her mother, "I should probably go upstairs. *Dat* wouldn't want me to cause a spectacle." Any more than she already had.

Her mother's open expression suggested she wanted to invite her daughter to partake in the day's service and meal, but she wouldn't go against her husband's wishes.

That wasn't the Amish way.

"It's okay, *Mem*," Bridget reassured her mother. "I found one of my old books in the wardrobe in a box." It had broken Bridget's heart to think of her mother tucking away a few of her daughter's things after she had run away. They were all harmless items, tokens from an innocent childhood. However, the likelihood of her father disposing of her possessions made her mother's efforts to hold on to them even more precious.

Zach hung back and watched the Amish women proceed into the barn, which had been converted into a place of worship, followed by the men, in some sort of prearranged order. Then a few stragglers, including teenagers, picked up the rear. Bridget's grandfather Jeremiah had encouraged Zach to join them, assuring him that visitors were welcome. However, Zach hadn't been inside a church building since he was a young boy, and he wasn't going to start now, even if it was a barn. Besides, he felt more comfortable as an observer of all the comers and goers. So far, they all seemed to be Amish people. No threat to Bridget. Since they were all dressed the same, she truly blended in.

He had scanned the faces of the women, wondering if Bridget would join her community. But she was a no-show. After a deep melodic singing began, he walked toward the house. Jeremiah had warned him that the service could last three hours. He entered the empty house and called out to her and heard a rustling upstairs. A few moments later, she came downstairs.

"Oh, it's you." Her shoulders visibly sagged. She tore off her bonnet and adjusted a bobby pin in her hair then put the bonnet back on. "Is something wrong?"

"Skipping the service?" He leaned against one of the support beams in the center of the room.

"My father forbade it." Despite the severity of the claim, there was a light quality to her voice.

"I'd think they'd be happy that you're home. That they'd want you to go to the service with them."

Bridget held on to the pine handrail and lowered herself to a seated position on one of the bottom stairs. Her bare feet with pink toes stuck out from her long dress. "My *dat* has to make everyone think he's mad at me. I may never know how he really feels. He's the head of this family, and they look up to him to determine how to act. However, the rules aren't up to him. The Amish believe in the ultimate form of tough love. If they shun me and keep me 'separate'—" she lifted her fingers in air quotes for the last word "—the hope is that I'll see the error of my ways and ask for forgiveness. My *dat* can't appear to be accepting of my transgressions. It would set a bad example for my siblings."

"Ah," Zach said. "I guess I should have asked you more questions about your living situation before I brought you here." However, being strict wasn't the worst crime. Being neglectful and absent were far worse. Many of the young men he came across in gangs had been largely ignored by their families.

"I knew what I was in for when I agreed to come home."

"It's a shame." Her father's punitive nature seemed overly harsh, especially toward a young woman who was making a good life for herself. Perhaps they didn't realize the real trouble people could get into. How would her parents have reacted to a daughter like Leann, someone addicted to drugs? He supposed everyone had to follow their own path and make their own mistakes, including shunning a perfectly decent person.

Bridget sagged and rested her head on the edge of the

railing post. She played with the strings on her bonnet. "It's what they know. They want to guilt me into returning."

Zach plucked at his suspenders. "It's hot in here. Would you like to talk a walk? Get some fresh air?"

Bridget pulled herself up to standing. "I'd love it." She spun around and took the stairs two at a time. "Let me put on my boots," she called over her shoulder. "I'll meet you out back."

Bridget had made herself presentable—by Amish standards—before heading outside. She figured they had a solid three hours before the service in the barn ended. As she and Zach crossed the field, she lifted her face toward the sun and bit back the automatic tendency to fill the silence with talk about the weather. After all the excitement of the past couple days, she wanted to try to just be. Enjoy the moment. Enjoy this glorious late-summer Sunday morning.

Zach walked by her side, allowing her to lead the way. She followed a familiar path that wound for a few hundred yards into the trees, around a man-made lake, then to the far side of the barn. Then they could cut across the field to the house. Zach could leave and she'd retreat to her bedroom and pray that someone thought to bring her some food.

They reached the tree line, and the dappled sunlight created dancing shadows. An earthy smell reached her nose and took her right back. It was surreal. The Miller kids had spent hours playing by the lake between their chores. When her little brothers weren't around, she and Liddie used to talk about the husbands they'd have, their homes and children. Liddie never had any reason to believe that it wouldn't come to fruition. Bridget had believed it, too, at first, because leaving seemed like too big of a leap. Until staying became more of one.

"I thought I'd spend my entire life here," Bridget said, no longer wanting to be alone with her thoughts.

"What made you decide to leave? I'm starting to see how hard that must have been." Zach slowed and squinted against the sun streaming through the trees.

"You should have grabbed a hat."

Half his mouth quirked up, making him more handsome. "I'm more of a baseball hat kinda guy. The straw hat was making my head itch." The power of suggestion made him scratch his head.

"The hat might have been too small." She resisted a strange urge to run her fingers along the subtle red line marking his forehead where the hat had sat. Lacing her fingers, she added, "I'm pretty impressed the clothes fit, though."

She reached up and plucked a yellowish-green leaf off the maple tree. In a couple months, they'd be vibrant red. She twirled the stem between her fingers, her mind traveling back to the time when the idea that her vocation might be outside this patch of dirt.

"I can't get used to not having pockets." Zach ran his thumbs under his suspenders. "I had to leave my wallet in the glove box."

Bridget laughed. Despite the tough-guy vibe she had initially gotten from him at the coffee shop, she was sensing something else. A soft heart somewhere deep down, one he seemed to be fighting hard to protect.

Maybe she should share with him why she had left. It might make him realize how important it was that she get back to Buffalo for the start of classes in a week. She had to complete her nursing degree. "When I was around fourteen, my *mem* was expecting another baby."

Zach stopped and turned to face her, obviously sensing she was about to share something important with him.

She smiled up at him, hoping to stop the heat crawling up her neck. "My *dat* was away at an auction overnight," she continued, her pulse thrumming in her ears. Zach's expression remained neutral. "She wasn't due to have the baby for another two months. She went into labor early. I had to help her deliver the baby."

"That's incredible. At fourteen?"

"*Yah*, well, I didn't know what to do. My mother was feverish. The baby was so tiny. I sent Liddie down the road to call an ambulance. I left Liddie with the younger kids and went with my mom to the hospital." Bridget dropped the leaf and watched it float to the ground, landing on a dry patch of dirt. She started walking again and Zach held back a branch so she could pass.

"They saved my *mem*." She sniffed. "My brother didn't make it." She worked her lower lip. "I overheard one of the doctors at the hospital say the baby would have had a fighting chance if my mother had delivered in the hospital. Those words really stuck with me. It was the first time I had been in a hospital. I was fascinated with the men and women who devoted their lives to saving others." Bridget shrugged as if it were no big deal, but it was a very big deal, enough to make her leave everything she knew in Hickory Lane. "I wanted to be able to do that for someone."

"You couldn't do that here?" Zach asked.

"Not in the same way. Sure, we have midwives who help with births, but I wanted to be a nurse. I wanted to make sure my patients had every chance. The most advanced medical care." She cleared her throat. "Unlike my brother."

Bridget took another few steps, then looked up at him. For some reason, she suddenly felt the need to defend the Amish. "Don't get me wrong. We—or the Amish—do use hospitals when we have to. However, if I stayed here, I would have never been allowed to study to become a nurse. To have a career. I owe the life of my mother to those nurses who took care of her. And maybe if my brother had been born in a hospital…

"I felt so helpless. That day changed my life." Across the field, rows of buggies lined up. The horses had been set loose in the fenced-in field. "I had to leave everything I knew in order to become a nurse. It's been a long road. I had a lot of education to make up. We only go up to the eighth grade here."

"Why? Don't the Amish value education?"

"Education is something that could take a person away from the community." She shrugged. "You don't need more than an eighth-grade education to run a farm."

"Are all Amish farmers?"

"Not all of them. As land gets more precious, some of the men have had to find other jobs in factories or with building crews." She grabbed her skirt and stepped over a branch in the path.

"You're a very impressive woman." The admiration in Zach's voice made her blush.

"I don't know about that. Women you know have all sorts of impressive careers." Bridget's face blazed hotter. She wasn't sure why she said that.

"I've never met anyone like you." His deep voice washed over her, and she was glad she was a few steps ahead, where he couldn't see her face.

She found herself picking up her pace as they walked around the short side of the pond and reached the clearing. Seeing the barn and all the buggies gave her the courage to finally ask, "Do you think we could retrieve some of my things from my apartment?"

Zach caught up with her. "We can run to the store and

pick up whatever you need. You can't go back to the apartment. It's not safe. And, to be honest, a lot of your stuff was probably destroyed in the fire."

She stopped and tapped the toe of her boot on the hard earth. Hard-fought confidence straightened her spine. "But there's a chance some of the things were saved, right? Because I'm not talking about things I could easily replace at a store. I'd like to pick up my laptop and a few books."

One of his eyebrows drew down. "I could have an agent go to the apartment…"

"I'd like to go myself. See the damage and gather a few things. I was thinking last night, two of my classes next semester are online. This way if I'm a few days late starting the classes, I'll still be up-to-date with two of them. It'll make it easier to catch up."

"Someone could be watching the apartment."

She held her hand out to him, indicating his clothing. "You've proved to me you're good at undercover."

"More than you realize," he muttered.

"Well, we can sneak in. I can wear a baseball cap pulled low. Something. Somehow. Please?" Her voice grew high-pitched. "I can dress like a boy. Come on… There has to be a way."

Across the field, a young Amish woman emerged from the barn holding a toddler. Something about her frantic, jerky movements sent cold dread straight to Bridget's heart.

"Something's wrong." Without waiting a beat longer, Bridget raced across the field, frustrated that the fabric of her long dress tangled around her legs, slowed her down. She reached the woman, and another shock surged through her system.

"Katy!" Bridget's childhood friend was panic-stricken, jostling a toddler in her arms. The child's eyes were wide and her face was red. She was cramming her fist down her throat. Without waiting for permission, Bridget tugged the toddler from her mother's arms. "Did she have something in her mouth?"

"She had a handful of grapes. She was fussing. I thought the grapes would help her settle down." The Amish woman clasped her hands together and pressed them to her lips.

With tunnel-like focus, Bridget set the toddler on her feet and knelt down behind her. She gently leaned her forward, supporting her with one arm, and gave a solid back blow with the other. It didn't work. "Come on, little one." She tried again and again. On the third blow, the little girl threw up and then let out the most terrified cry. The child's arms swung up, reaching for her mother.

Bridget sat back on her heels and sagged with relief. *Thank You, God.* Zach placed his hand lightly on her shoulder. For the briefest of moments, she had forgotten he was there.

The commotion drew a few of the elders out of the barn. Bridget's heart stuttered when she recognized the bishop, silently taking in the situation.

Katy wept openly. She clung to her little girl and she held out her hand toward Bridget. "You saved my baby. *Denki, denki, denki.*"

The bishop met Bridget's gaze. If he was grateful or impressed, he didn't show it.

Mrs. Yoder ran out of the barn holding a smaller child. "What happened?"

"The baby was choking." Katy cupped her toddler's face and drew her to her chest and rocked back and forth, the relief evident on her pretty face.

"Oh…" Mrs. Yoder patted her granddaughter's head. She seemed to take note of the bishop. "Everything's okay.

Please go back in. I'll tend to my daughter and grand-daughter."

"Take the child to the house to get some water," the bishop said and turned with the others and went back to the barn.

"Come on," Bridget said. "I'll take you inside."

The toddler lifted her head and smiled through her tears. Bridget gently wiped a tear away from the little girl's cheek. "What's your name, honey?"

"Gracie." Katy smiled.

"Well, let's go get Gracie something to drink." Bridget met Zach's gaze. He nodded, and a small smile played on her lips.

Being proud wasn't a familiar trait of the Amish, and it wasn't one Bridget was used to. Right now, she was grateful she had been in the right place at the right time.

As they walked toward the house beside her childhood best friend, Zach leaned in and whispered, "You did great."

Bridget tipped her head. "If it wasn't me, it would have been someone else."

"Don't downplay what you did. That young mother left the barn because she didn't want her child to disrupt the service. Who knows what would have happened if you hadn't been here?" He gently placed his hand on the small of her back, directing her toward the house.

She shifted to say something to Zach, but then she saw her father lurking near the door of the barn like a storm cloud blowing in on the horizon.

Bridget settled Katy with Gracie in her lap on a rocker on the back porch and got them a drink of water. Mrs. Yoder stayed inside with the baby. Zach had disappeared. Bridget wondered why he hadn't said goodbye. She shoved aside the hint of disappointment and crouched down in front of her friend. She reached out to touch the toddler's bonnet string. "She's beautiful." She smiled up at her friend. "She has your eyes."

Katy pressed her cheek to her daughter's. "She has her father's feet." Her friend giggled, reminding Bridget of their childhood days.

"Did you marry Levi Shetler?"

Katy's cheeks turned pink. "*Yah*. You know Moses Lapp came back."

"He came back? From where?" Bridget fidgeted with Gracie's shoelace, then stood up and leaned back on the railing. Moses had been courting Bridget at the time she left Hickory Lane. He was a popular boy, and she'd assumed he'd move on to the next girl without missing a beat. After all, that was five years ago.

"Shortly after you left, he left, too. I thought you knew." She lowered her voice. "I guess you wouldn't."

"Where'd he go?" Curiosity got the best of her.

"There's a few rumors." Katy smiled with a flash of mischief in her eyes, then grew subdued. "I shouldn't repeat gossip." She wrapped her arms around Gracie, who was drifting off to sleep. "Liddie never mentioned him?" Bridget wrote off the odd lilt to her voice as the strain between two friends who hadn't seen each other in a long time.

"No, she never mentioned him," Bridget said. Moses had hung with the wilder crowd in Hickory Lane, but that was all relative. Everyone figured Bridget would have a calming presence after he started taking her home after the Sunday singings. "Is he married?" Bridget asked when the awkward silence had taken on a life of its own.

"*Neh*. I heard—"

"Are you going to come in and help or what?" Liddie appeared suddenly on the other side of the screen door.

She had slipped out of the service to help with the final preparations for the meal.

Bridget ran her palms down her cape. "I'm coming." She smiled at her friend. "Sorry, I have to go."

Katy reached out and touched Bridget's wrist. "Are you happy?"

Bridget frowned. "It's been a little stressful lately. I'm not sure how much you know." The Amish way of communication was old-fashioned but no less effective. When Katy didn't say anything, Bridget added, "I am happy."

"That's great." The positive sentiment sounded forced.

"Are you happy?" Even though Katy had been the first to ask, Bridget was genuinely curious. Katy was living the life that Bridget had given up. She was twenty-five. Married. And a mother. Other than her age, Bridget no longer had anything in common with her friend.

"I am happy." Katy hugged her daughter tight. "I can't thank you enough for helping Gracie."

Bridget squeezed the little girl's foot. "I'm glad I was there."

"Me too," Katy said. She straightened her daughter's dress over her socked foot. "I did hear the rumors about you. Does this mean you might be coming home?" The hope in her friend's voice broke her heart.

"Classes start next week. I'm going to be a nurse in nine months."

Katy paused a moment, as if reflecting, then said, "You're going to make a wonderful nurse, but I've missed you."

"I've missed you, too."

"I need help in here," Liddie called again, this time from deeper in the kitchen.

"One more thing..." Katy pressed her daughter's head

to her chest and covered her ear. "Why didn't you tell me you were leaving?"

"I didn't want to get you into trouble. I had to do it on my own." Bridget straightened. "You understand."

Katy kissed the top of her daughter's bonnet. "I do. I wished we could have talked about it."

"Bridget!" Liddie called again, this time with an edge of impatience.

Across the lawn, a sea of black clothes spilled out of the barn. The service was over. "You couldn't have talked me out of it."

Her friend looked up at her with wide eyes, as if Bridget had uncovered her darkest worry. That she hadn't recognized that her friend was unhappy and hadn't done something to make her want to stay. Bridget touched Katy's shoulder. "I need to go before Liddie short-sheets my bed."

Katy laughed. "Go. And promise me you'll come by before you leave next time."

"I will." Bridget slipped inside the door. Liddie was nowhere to be seen.

"Everyone okay?" Zach appeared in the kitchen doorway.

"Yes." Especially now that Bridget realized Zach was still here. She peeled the foil off a dish. The sweet smell of red peppers and olive oil made her stomach growl.

"Need help?" Zach asked.

"I thought you wanted to blend in."

He furrowed his brow, clearly not understanding.

"You can't blend in if you hang out in the kitchen." She lifted one skeptical eyebrow. Was this his idea of working undercover? "Go outside and find my grandfather. He'll be happy to share a meal with you."

"I will." Zach stepped closer and lowered his voice. "I made a few phone calls. We can get you back inside your apartment to grab a few things. Looks like the fire department did a good job."

Bridget spun around and, in her excitement, she stumbled forward and planted her hands on his chest. He placed his hands on her hips to steady her, then quickly dropped them to his side.

The sound of someone clearing his throat drew their attention. Her father stood in the doorway. "I will not tolerate your being disrespectful under my roof."

Bridget's face burned from embarrassment. "I wasn't… I didn't…" She bowed her head and turned around and fussed with the cling wrap covering a plate of chocolate chip cookies. "I should probably set out the food."

"No disrespect meant, sir," Zach said. "I was headed outside. Is there anything I could do for you?"

Her father seemed taken aback, an expression Bridget rarely saw on his face. He seemed to be debating, then finally he said, "The young men are carrying the benches out of the barn and rearranging them into tables on the lawn. Perhaps they could use a hand."

"Of course," Zach said, then to Bridget, "I'll be outside if you need me."

Before Bridget had a chance to form the right words, her father had slipped back out the door. A moment later her mother breezed in. "Everyone's saying you saved baby Gracie. Is that something you learned in school?" Her mother's voice sounded reverent.

"I didn't mean to draw attention to myself. I was taking a walk when Katy came outside. Her baby was choking."

Her mother surprised her by smiling. "*Gott* put you where you were needed."

Bridget nodded, unable to speak as emotion clogged her throat. She wanted nothing more than to be back on her mother's good side. Her father's, too. But that would never happen if she wanted to become a nurse. And she'd never be able to become a nurse if she stayed in Hickory Lane.

NINE

Early Monday morning, Bridget and Zach headed into Buffalo. Bridget had hardly slept last night wondering if her *dat* would try to stop her at the door, if her things at the apartment had been damaged beyond repair, if she was naively putting herself and Zach in danger. If…if… if… Her worries nagged at her until the first signs of dawn dragged her out of bed. She stuffed her *Englisch* clothes into a cloth tote and almost made it out of her childhood bedroom before Liddie sat up and begged to tag along. Definitely not. Then Bridget said goodbye to her *mem* in the kitchen, promising she'd be back later today, and slipped out while her father was in the barn. She'd deal with his anger later.

From the passenger seat of Zach's truck, Bridget stared at the stately buildings of the University at Buffalo's Main Street campus on the way to the DEA office downtown. Apparently, Zach's supervisor wanted a statement in person before they swung by her apartment. Bridget pressed a hand to her midsection and gulped air, hoping her nerve-induced nausea would pass. She focused hard on the college campus outside her window, imagining it buzzing with students, and she prayed by this time next week she would be one of them. It had been a long, hard road to get here, and she could *not* give up now.

Once the campus was out of view, Bridget shifted in her seat to face Zach. "Thanks for taking the long way downtown."

"Yeah, sure, no problem. I enjoy taking Main Street downtown every so often. I love this city." She would have heard the smile in his voice even if she hadn't been looking at him.

The tension of yesterday began to fall away. Her father had barely spoken two words after his initial admonishment for daring to be seen, forget that she'd helped sweet little Gracie. His body language spoke volumes. He was brimming with agitation that he wasn't able to control his older daughter. Yet she loved the man. He was her father. He was also a product of the community in which he lived, and he truly believed he was doing the best thing for his daughter and his family in the eyes of God.

Did he really think his tough love would bring her back for good? Would he ever accept that God was bigger than their small Amish community? That she could serve Him and be a nurse?

She rubbed her forehead, trying to stop the constant barrage of concerns that threatened to give her a headache.

"You okay?" Zach cut her a quick glance. The warm concern in his eyes softened the edges of her worries.

"I'm fine." She fidgeted with the zipper on her hoodie. The morning chill signaling the approaching end of summer would burn off soon. They had stopped at a rest area outside Hickory Lane so she could put on *Englisch* clothes. She wished changing her mind-set was as easy as switching her plain black boots for her favorite sneakers.

"You know, I didn't intentionally spring this trip to the DEA offices on you. It wasn't a bait and switch." He laughed, a mirthless sound. "My supervisor called me late last night. They want to get an official statement from you, and since we were already planning a trip into town, I set it up. Things are moving fast. We'll head to your apartment right after. I promise." Zach slowed at the red light.

"I know," Bridget said quietly. "I trust you." She did, even after only knowing him a few days.

A little while later, Zach pulled into a parking spot near a building with beautiful architectural detail. Bridget often found herself staring at the buildings in downtown Buffalo. The massive structures were unlike anything she knew growing up. They hustled toward the door and took the elevator up to his office and into a large conference room with floor-to-ceiling windows overlooking the city. She took in the view. Beautiful.

A few moments later, a smartly dressed woman came into the room with a laptop tucked under her arm. She smiled, more businesslike than friendly and she offered her hand. "Hello, I'm Assistant Special Agent in Charge Colleen McCarthy." She slipped in front of a chair and pushed it back with her knee, set her laptop down on the large conference table and sat down. She held out her palm to Bridget. "Have a seat. We appreciate your cooperation. This shouldn't take too long."

Zach closed the conference room door after Bridget asked to be excused following an intense interrogation. He turned and faced his supervisor with his hands on his hips. "Did you need to be that hard on her? She's not involved. She's the one who reported the activity."

His supervisor, ASAC McCarthy, snapped closed her laptop and swiveled in her seat to face him. "First of all, you are supposed to be on leave. We talked about this."

Zach pulled out a chair and sat down. He rolled it toward his boss and rested his forearms on his thighs. "I can't leave this woman high and dry. She trusts me."

"Listen—" Colleen leaned back, resting one elbow on the table next to her "—you delivered her to safety at her family's Amish farm." One brow dipped down at the word *Amish*. "She's good. Now you need to take a break. I can't risk losing one of my best agents."

"She's in danger. Her coworker was murdered." He straightened and crossed his arms over his chest. "Any word on that investigation?"

Colleen hesitated for a moment. "Ashley Meadows was attacked on the running trail near the university."

"Cause of death?"

"Strangulation." She paused a beat, then said, "We're going to get this guy. I promise."

Zach scratched the back of his head. He should have done more sooner. He cleared his throat. "What about the Kevin Pearson investigation?" Kevin was his confidential informant who had been shot last week. Zach worked day in and day out in a stressful job, but the past few weeks had been the worst of his career.

"Nothing yet." Colleen relaxed her posture and leaned forward. "You have to let it go. You'll be cleared."

Zach shook his head, deep in thought. Had he put too much pressure on the kid? Kevin had claimed he was getting clean and only hung around the bar because he felt like he had a purpose helping Zach take down his suppliers. That was the goal: get the little fish on the hook to reel in the big ones. Didn't always work out.

"I should have pulled the plug," Zach said, turning to stare out over the Buffalo skyline. He had regretted not getting the kid out, but that hadn't been his decision, nor had it been his job. His job was to use the little guy to get the big guy. Otherwise, the Kevins of the world could just be replaced. He scrubbed a hand across his face. It still didn't make it any easier.

"Don't do this to yourself," Colleen said. "You've got to take a break. Get your head straight. Put that incident behind you. I'm confident you'll be cleared of wrongdoing, and I can't have you coming back to work second-guessing yourself." Half her mouth quirked up. "I need my take-charge agent back here once you're cleared. You have to take Bridget back to Hickory Lane and get out of there. That's an order."

Colleen must have read something in his expression, because she narrowed her eyes and leaned closer. "I've never known you to let a case get personal."

"Kevin was just a kid. Maybe I pushed him too hard."

"I wasn't talking about your CI."

"You're talking about Bridget? It's not personal." He returned her unflinching gaze, proving he meant it. No one had ever accused him of not knowing how to play a role. Going deep undercover. Pretending.

"Are you sure?" Colleen tilted her head and paused before standing.

Zach studied the industrial-gray carpet. *How do I really feel?*

He had been stuffing down the feelings that had sparked the moment he first noticed Bridget sitting alone in the coffee shop. Ashley had sent him a photo. But he hadn't expected to feel something. Her gentle nature was soothing to his battered soul. Most of the people he dealt with through work had a pent-up energy that kept him on high alert. Something about her threatened his carefully guarded heart.

Or maybe he really was simply run-down and vulnerable.

Colleen picked up her laptop from the conference table and tucked it under her arm. "You look beat."

Zach's smile sneaked up on him. "The haggard look is usually an asset." Working undercover had been his primary gig the past four years. None of his druggie associates ever accused him of looking tired, probably because most of them saw the world through heavily lidded eyes.

"You don't need to babysit Bridget."

Babysit.

Zach ran the back of his fist across his mouth. "She's pretty skittish. I'd hate to scare her off."

Colleen shifted her laptop to her other arm. "She gave her official statement. I'm not sure how much more we need. We've been through this before. Far too often. Once the forensic analysts go through the records at the clinic, they'll determine if they can issue an immediate suspension order. The good doctor—even when they find him—won't have the ability to prescribe controlled substances. You know how this works."

He did. "Any updates?" Hovering around the periphery of an investigation wasn't familiar to him.

"Frank—" another agent in the office "—put a call in to the Philadelphia police department. The good doctor apparently doesn't believe in cash. Lucky for us. He used his credit card at a hotel. So, unless he realizes his mistake and bolts, we should have him in custody any moment now."

"Why didn't you tell me this the minute I got here?" Zach asked.

"Because you're on leave." Colleen pressed her lips together and opened her eyes wide. "You're one of my best agents. I need you back here whole once you're cleared."

Bridget needed him, too. "I think I should stick close to Bridget. Her friend was killed. Bridget was nearly run down. Her house was firebombed." Zach ticked the items off on his fingers.

"Who's going to find her in Hickory Lane?" She shifted

YOU pick your books – WE pay for everything.

You get up to FOUR New Books and TWO Mystery Gifts...absolutely FREE

Dear Reader,

I am writing to announce the launch of a huge **FREE BOOK GIVEAWAY**... and to let you know that YOU are entitled to choose up to FOUR fantastic books that WE pay for.

Try **Love Inspired® Romance Larger-Print** books and fall in love with inspirational romances that take you on an uplifting journey of faith, forgiveness and hope.

Try **Love Inspired® Suspense Larger-Print** books where courage and optimism unite in stories of faith and love in the face of danger.

Or TRY BOTH!

In return, we ask just one favor: Would you please participate in our brief Reader Survey? We'd love to hear from you.

This FREE BOOK GIVEAWAY means that we pay for *everything!* We'll even cover the shipping, and no purchase is necessary, now or later. So please return your survey today. You'll get **Two Free Books** and **Two Mystery Gifts** from each series to try, altogether worth over **$20!**

Sincerely

Pam Powers

Pam Powers
For Harlequin Reader Service

Complete the survey below and return it today to receive up to 4 FREE BOOKS and FREE GIFTS guaranteed!

HARLEQUIN READER SERVICE—Here's how it works:

her weight and gave him the "how many times do we have to go through this?" stare.

"Don't we owe her something?" Zach bit out. "She came forward with her report."

His supervisor's expression was inscrutable. She didn't get to where she was by being soft.

"Bridget deserves more respect than to be told to sit tight while we figure this out. She's a college student. She wants to start classes next week."

"Her safety is top priority. She's going to have to be patient. But there's no reason you have to stay in Hickory Lane, too. It's a perfect safe house."

When he didn't answer, Colleen tipped her head. "Do you have any reason to believe she's not safe in Hickory Lane?"

"No." The single word came out clipped.

"Then there's your answer. No need to take it personally, Zach." Colleen tapped his forearm with a soft fist bump before opening the conference room door. Bridget was standing on the other side. Based on her flushed face, he didn't need to ask if she overheard their conversation.

"Ready to go?" Zach stepped into the corridor, walls lined with photographs of long-retired agents.

"Sure." She ran a hand over her ponytail in what he now recognized as a nervous gesture.

"We'll keep you updated on the investigation," his supervisor said, holding her laptop to her chest. "Thank you for coming in."

"I had to," Bridget said. "What they're doing is wrong."

When they reached the bottom of the stairwell, Bridget turned to him. "What now?"

"Let's run by your apartment and get your things."

"Do you really think it's okay?" She dropped her hand from playing with her hair.

"You're not getting cold feet on me now, are you?" He tried to make light of the situation.

"No, no," Bridget said, not sounding very convincing.

Maybe once Bridget had her laptop and textbooks, she wouldn't mind being left alone in Hickory Lane.

TEN

About a block from Bridget's apartment, Zach pulled his truck over. He reached into the back seat and grabbed a Buffalo Bills baseball cap and offered it to her. "Do you think you can stuff your hair into this?"

She began twisting her ponytail into a high bun. "Can't be harder than fitting it under a bonnet, right?"

"Yeah," Zach said distractedly. He craned his neck to check his surroundings, it seemed. "Got it?" His attention landed on Bridget stuffing the last bit of hair up into the baseball cap. His steely gaze made a chill run up her spine.

"I'm all set." She pulled the bill of the hat low on her forehead.

"Maybe I should run up to your apartment and leave you in the truck."

Disappointment edged out her apprehension. "Please, I want to go in. I need to search for a few things, if that's okay with you."

His eyes stared, unseeing. His shoulders sagged a fraction, and she knew he'd relented. "We have to hurry." The seriousness of his tone set her teeth on edge. Did he really think someone was waiting for her?

Bridget gave him a quick nod. With that, Zach drove to a parking lot across the street from her apartment complex, and they got out and walked the long way around to her unit. They both wore ball caps, looking like they were ready to go to the team's home opener, not that she'd know from experience.

They strode through the courtyard. Her eye was drawn to the emergency-closure boards nailed to the frame of her bedroom window. In the middle of the day, the area was deserted. Most of her neighbors were at work, making it easier for her and Zach to sneak in and out unnoticed. Bridget jogged up the stairs, and Zach followed close behind. With key in hand, Bridget approached her apartment door. Her mind flashed back to the first time she had gotten the keys to her very own place. Her very first tangible evidence of freedom.

Poof. Gone.

The key slipped in her sweaty fingers.

You can do this.

The key slid into the lock, and she heard the solid click of the dead bolt retracting. She pushed open the door, and the dank air hung thick with smoke and dampness. It was a far cry from the scent of the lavender air freshener she loved.

Zach entered the room behind her. "Get what you need. I'll wait here. And hurry."

A lump of emotion made it impossible to speak. Bridget walked through the untouched family room to her bedroom. She opened the door and slid her hand along the wall, reaching for the light switch and flicked it back and forth. Nothing. The only source of light was from the hallway since boards covered the windows, leaving the room cast in heavy shadows and making it seem smaller. The cloying scent didn't help.

"The electricity has probably been shut off because of

the fire," Zach called from the living room. "Do you have your phone on you? Use the flashlight app."

Bridget directed the beam around the bedroom. Gingerly she fingered her pink comforter, now charred and damp from the fire and subsequent firefighting efforts. Suddenly she felt very tired. Exhausted. Had all the challenges she had faced to get here been for nothing? Tonight, she'd be back in her bed in Hickory Lane with no real timeline for returning to Buffalo.

"Did you find what you needed?" Zach hollered from the other room. "We should get going."

Zach's impatience made her nervous. She scanned the beam of light around the room. She peeled back the closet doors and found her backpack. It seemed to be mostly untouched by the flames, and the nylon had protected it from the water. She hoisted it onto her shoulder. She grabbed a couple textbooks from the top shelf of the closet. Then she found her notebook and favorite pens in her desk drawer. The pages of the notebook were a little wavy from the dampness. She shook her head to try to dispel the constant unease that made her skin buzz. She had her laptop and books. She'd be able to keep up with two online classes.

She backed out and scanned the room one last time, the light from her smartphone touching on the life she had made here for the past couple years after she moved off campus. The life that clearly no longer existed. Even if—no when—she returned permanently, this wouldn't be her home. She'd never be able to live here again without reliving the explosive crash and fire.

She turned off the flashlight and balanced the phone on the textbooks in her arms. She pulled her bedroom door closed out of habit.

"Got everything?" Zach opened the outside door a fraction.

"Almost." Bridget ducked into the kitchen to grab her migraine meds. Just then, a commotion sounded in the next room. She poked her head out of the kitchen to find Dr. Ryan pointing a gun at Zach and forcing him back into her apartment. Her heart dropped.

Instinctively, she backed up while clutching her things. Zach lifted his hands and seemed to be trying to tell her something with his keen gaze.

Her boss pushed the door closed with his foot. "Why did you have to do this?"

Bridget's gaze moved from Dr. Ryan to Zach and back. Zach shook his head slightly. Taking his cue, she stayed quiet.

"Dr. Ryan, it's over," Zach said.

The physician scoffed. "For who? I'm the one holding the gun."

"Killing isn't in your nature. You're a healer."

Her boss seemed to blanch.

Zach held out his palm. "Hand me your weapon. This ends here."

The physician seemed to consider this for a moment before shaking his head. He glared at Bridget. She had never seen him this angry. He always had a wonderful bedside manner, and only once had she heard him get upset with one of his employees. The nighttime janitor had accidentally left the alley door unlocked. Anything could have been stolen. Yet the doctor himself had been the biggest threat to the clinic.

"It should never have gone this far," the physician said ruefully. "Why didn't you mind your own business?" Dr. Ryan scrubbed a hand over his face and shuddered. "You and Ashley should have minded your own business."

"Ashley..." The single word slipped out of Bridget's lips. Her mouth felt dry. "You killed Ashley."

"Bridget…" Zach warned.

Something flashed in the doctor's eyes. "I didn't mean… She wouldn't listen."

"You don't want this to go any further," Zach said, his voice calm yet authoritative.

Bridget's boss turned, and in one swift motion, Zach disarmed him and had the man's face pressed against the wall.

Bridget slid down the wall to the floor, sagging with relief and finally letting the tears fall.

"You okay?" Zach asked, pressing his knee into Seth Ryan's back and yanking his arm up in the most uncomfortable position.

Bridget nodded and set her things on the floor next to her. She swiped at a tear running down her cheek.

"Any chance you have a zip tie in that kitchen of yours?"

"Yeah." Bridget got to her feet and ran to the kitchen. He could hear her opening and closing drawers until she returned with a black zip tie. "This?"

"Perfect." He took the plastic zip tie and wrapped it around the doctor's wrists and cranked it tight. The doctor grunted. The fasteners should hold, because the doctor didn't have much fight left in him. Zach grabbed the doctor's arm and dragged him a few feet, letting him sit with his back against the wall. "Who's down in Philly?" The DEA had tracked his credit card to a hotel down there.

Seth's eyes narrowed, and he shook his head. It seemed the doctor wasn't going to talk. Instead, he bowed his head and sobbed, loudly and with little dignity.

Zach joined Bridget, who was sitting on the edge of the couch shaking. She looked up at him, and he reached out and took her hand.

"Is it over?"

He wanted more than anything to say yes, but he knew that wasn't true. In his experience, each of these guys was just a cog in the wheel. "Hang tight. I'm going to call this in."

She exhaled a long, shaky breath. "Okay."

It didn't take long for a Buffalo police officer to come pick up Seth Ryan, then Zach turned to Bridget. "Let me get you home."

"Home?" she asked when they were alone again. She straightened the footstool that had been jostled in the skirmish.

"Not here. You need to go back to Hickory Lane until we finish our investigation. It shouldn't be long." He wasn't sure if the last bit was a white lie or not. Either way, he needed to reassure her.

"Are you going to drop me off and leave? I overheard you talking to your supervisor."

The protest died on his lips. Bridget shrugged, seeming so frail and thin. "I get it." She sniffed. "With Dr. Ryan in custody, the case should be over soon, right? Besides, you have better things to do than babysit me."

Inwardly he winced at her choice of words. The same ones his supervisor had used in the office. They lacked respect. "Come on." He held out his hand, and she accepted it, coming to her feet. How could he explain to her that these cases were never cut-and-dried? "We don't know who else is in involved, but this is a huge start. Huge. Okay?"

"Okay…"

"I want you to go back to Hickory Lane for a few more days, at least."

"Alone, right?" Her dejected tone suggested she already knew the answer.

"I'll make sure you get settled."

Bridget hoisted her backpack on her shoulder and picked up the items she had set on the floor. "Let's go."

Shortly after they got into the truck, his cell phone rang. His mother's name flashed on the caller ID on his dash. He hit Ignore. A moment later, it rang again.

"Go ahead and answer it," Bridget said.

His thumb hovered over Ignore before curiosity got the best of him. "Hello." He hadn't taken a call from his mother in over two years. The last time she'd been slurring her words and berated him. He hadn't stayed on the phone long enough to find out why she had been all bent out of shape.

"Zachary, it's your mother." Her voice cracked over the line, filling the inside of the cab. She sounded tired but clear. Sober. He tightened his grip on the steering wheel.

"How can I help you?" Realizing how formal he sounded, he was acutely aware of Bridget's presence.

Her mother sniffed. "I heard about Ashley. Poor, sweet girl…" She went quiet before finding her voice again. "I saw her not that long ago. I gave her your business card. Did she call you?"

Zach rested his elbow on the door and rubbed his forehead. "She called me." He cleared his throat. "Did you read about her death in the paper?"

"You know I don't get the newspaper."

Actually, he didn't know. He had moved out of his mother's house when he was eighteen for college. From there, he'd enlisted. He'd avoided his childhood at all costs, including his baby sister.

"Ashley's parents told me. They said she was murdered." His mother emphasized the word *murdered* as if it were offensive solely to her. "Her poor mother. I did what I could to comfort her, you know, one mother to another who lost a child. Only another mother could understand that."

Growing anger bubbled in his gut. His mother loved

the martyr card. What she failed to acknowledge was that she'd been too strung out to recognize the same symptoms in her own daughter. He gritted his teeth to avoid saying something he'd later regret. "Is there anything else? I have work to do."

"Always work…"

He checked the traffic before turning right. "Well, there's a lot of drugs out there." He couldn't help the dig.

"If you took the time to visit me, you'd know I've changed," his mother said, her voice growing soft.

Not soon enough. Bridget stared out the passenger window. "I have to go. Please express my condolences to the Meadows family."

"Goodbye, Zachary." His mother's tone was resigned. "It's obvious that you don't have time for me."

Zach ended the call. Silence hung thick and heavy in the air.

Bridget shifted in her seat. "You're estranged from your family, too."

He hitched a shoulder. "My mother always chose drugs over us."

"Now you're doing the same." Bridget sounded faraway.

"I'm on the right side of the law." A hard edge sharpened his words. Zach turned on his directional and took the on-ramp to the Thruway.

"How do you suppose Dr. Ryan found us so quickly?" Bridget's abrupt change in conversation caught Zach off guard. He checked the rearview mirror. He had been careful to take a circuitous route before he got on the Thruway, and he planned to get off an exit or two after the one to Hickory Lane and then double back. He couldn't be too careful.

"They'll look into that. My guess, someone close by was watching the apartment." He cleared his throat. "That's why I was reluctant to take you there." He sensed Bridget was about to apologize, so he held up his hand. "In the end, going back there was a great way to flush him out. Ideally, I would have had an agent go in with me, not a civilian. Thankfully it all worked out. Now we have him in custody."

"Why do you think he did it?" Bridget asked. "I thought he was a good man."

"I'm sure we'll find out now that he's in custody."

Bridget let out a long breath. "How long will it take before I can come back to Buffalo for good?"

"Analysts are going through the records and the videos of people coming and going from the clinic. The Buffalo Police Department is investigating Ashley's death. With more than one crime scene, the pieces will come together. Quickly." Zach reached out to pat her on the knee, then thought better of it. "And now they have the doctor in custody. It shouldn't be long."

The protective shield he had built around his heart was crumbling. His heart ached for Bridget. The pain on her face made it evident that his confident reassurances meant little to her.

His mind flashed to the good doctor sobbing in the apartment. The compassion that he might have felt for a life ruined was replaced by hot anger at the lives destroyed in greed's wake.

ELEVEN

Bridget's twelve-year-old brother, Caleb, came charging across the field backlit by bold streaks of orange and purple in a glorious evening sky. If Bridget were to list the things she missed about Hickory Lane, the sunset would be near the top, somewhere after her family and the gentle quiet. She *really* missed the quiet.

Her little brother pulled up short, apparently embarrassed by his enthusiasm. "You came back," he said with an air of disbelief.

Bridget's heart broke for her sweet little brother. He had been only seven when she left Hickory Lane to become a nurse. They had been especially close. She'd read to him, helped him sound out words, determined to make him a strong reader. Her parents shrugged off his struggles. It was her own quiet rebellion. Little did her family know that soon she'd be committing the ultimate rebellion by leaving.

Bridget planted her hand on Caleb's shoulder, not wanting to embarrass him by a full-on hug. The Amish weren't much for displays of emotion. "I'm back." She left out the words *for now.* She had no stomach for conflict or making others feel bad. That's probably why she had initially been reluctant to report her suspicions about the clinic. Even now, thinking about Dr. Ryan being led out by the police made her heart break for his family. How had a man gone so wrong?

Bridget made a show of swatting at a mosquito. "Let's get moving before I get eaten alive." The three of them continued to traipse across the field. Bridget had her backpack hoisted up on her shoulder. It must have made an odd sight with her plain clothes. Zach hadn't bothered to change because he was leaving. This definitive announcement was like a sucker punch to the gut.

Seemingly satisfied that his sister hadn't left him for good, Caleb ran ahead to the house. He picked up a volleyball on the way and tossed it up in the air and caught it. When Bridget reached the house, she turned to Zach. There was so much she wanted to say—Would she see him again? Would he let her know when it was safe to come home? Was he going to reach out to his mom?—but all she could muster was, "Thank you for taking me to my apartment to get my things."

"And we smoked out the good doctor." A smile tilted the corners of his mouth. She was going to miss that handsome face.

"Kinda like he initially smoked me out?" She pressed her lips together. "I still can't believe he was involved with all this. He was such a good man." Bridget held her crossed arms close.

"People make bad choices." He tilted his head to look into her eyes. "You made the right one. Don't ever doubt that."

Bridget nodded, slowly. Still not entirely convinced. "I'm going to miss the entire semester, aren't I?" Pinpricks of anxiety reached every corner of her scalp. Despite having her laptop and her books, if she couldn't return to campus, she'd inevitably fall behind. She blinked rapidly, then consciously tried to slow down her thoughts, her breath. This was only meant to be temporary.

Zach placed his hand on hers, stilling her fluttering motions. "I won't leave you here longer than necessary. I'll call when it's safe. I'll send someone to get you."

Disappointment crushed her heart. *He'll send someone?* Of course he'd send someone. She had no right to expect it to be him. He worked in a big office with lots of people. Forcing a smile to hide the hurt, she settled on a simple "Thank you."

Zach leaned closer; a soft smile played on his lips. He smelled of aloe and mint. Her face grew flushed, and he pulled his head back a fraction. "Would you mind if I kissed you?"

Her mind went blank. All she could do was give her head a slight nod in the affirmative.

He reached out and cupped her cheek, his hand both strong and gentle. He leaned in again, and this time she closed her eyes. His warm lips brushed ever so softly across hers. Tingles of awareness rushed through her body. Slowly, she opened her eyes. He had a sad smile on his face.

"I'm going to miss you."

"Yeah."

"Maybe if circumstances had been different…" He searched her face.

"Yeah." *Say something more.*

"You're going to make a great nurse. Don't ever give up on that dream."

"I won't." Her heart beat wildly, drowning out her soft voice.

"Well…" Zach took a step backward. "I'm going to grab something I left at your grandfather's. Then I'm driving home. I'll be in touch."

"Okay, sure." She waved, feeling self-conscious. "'Night," she said, more enthusiastically than she felt. Afraid her emotions were going to get the best of her, Bridget slipped into the house and went right upstairs.

She was surprised to find Liddie fumbling with something in the closet. She seemed startled when Bridget called her name. Her younger sister spun around. "Did anyone ever tell you not to sneak up on someone?" She laughed nervously. Then her shoulders slowly slid down from her ears. "You're home."

"I am." Bridget plopped her backpack on the bed, tempted to gush about what had just happened. A bigger part of her wanted to keep it to herself. A cherished memory.

"How'd it go?"

"Fine." She wasn't ready to tell her sister everything. Talk of the doctor's arrest would obliterate the warm and fuzzies she was still enjoying from her last interaction with Zach. "I had to make an official report before we went to my apartment." She sounded normal, right? No sign that a handsome man had sent her pulse into overdrive with the most innocent of kisses. She rubbed the back of her neck and smiled to herself.

"Glad you had a good trip, even without me," Liddie said, sounding like a petulant child.

"It was a quick visit." Bridget unzipped her backpack and pulled out her computer.

"Wait." Liddie narrowed her gaze. "Why do you have that funny smile?"

Bridget quickly schooled her expression and shrugged. She patted her laptop, eager to change the subject. "I need this for school. I should probably tuck it away so *Dat* doesn't get mad?"

Liddie held up a finger and spun around and opened the

wardrobe. She unfolded the top layer of a blanket on the bottom shelf. "Tuck it in here." Liddie unfolded another blanket, revealing her cell phone.

Bridget met her sister's excited gaze with concern. "How long are you going to keep this phone?"

Liddie smirked. "I don't think you should be telling me what I can or cannot do."

"You're right." Bridget couldn't be a hypocrite. Hopefully, Liddie would find her way through *Rumspringa* and emerge on the other side, the adult she was meant to be. Funny, Bridget was still struggling with finding her place.

Did it include Zach? No, not possible. His life was undercover work. Her sole focus was school and beyond that, a career in nursing.

Bridget placed her laptop on the blanket in Liddie's arms. Her sister folded the material over the top and then tucked the package in the bottom of their wardrobe. "I suppose we'll have to find another hiding place once it gets cold and we need the blanket." She shrugged. "Works for now."

How long did her sister think she was staying? A hint of nostalgia burned the back of her nose. Bridget was already missing these days. Missing this day in particular. She cleared her throat and decided for however many days she had left in Hickory Lane, she'd try to stay present.

Liddie flopped down on her bed and crossed her legs at the ankles, and twirled her bare feet. They were black on the bottom. "Did you figure out how you are going to charge your laptop?"

Bridget laughed. "I'm hoping I'll be back in Buffalo before classes start, but if I'm not, I'll have to go into town and use the Wi-Fi and electricity at the coffee shop."

"Wait till the tourists get a photo of you in your bonnet on your laptop." Liddie stared at her with an amused expression. She shook her head, as if dismissing the idea. "Grandfather has a generator. I'm sure he'd let you charge your laptop."

"Good to know. Thanks." Bridget sat down on the opposite twin bed, the one she had slept in as a child. The one where she'd lain wide-awake planning her uncertain future and then secretly crying with self-doubt and indecision.

"One day at a time." Bridget threw out the cliché to hide her frustration that she hadn't had time to think any of this through. Maybe she should chase down Zach and beg him to take her back to Buffalo, because the unknown certainty she faced in Buffalo seemed less scary than the familiar side-eye and cool glares she'd face here.

Is that the only reason you want to chase Zach down?

She laughed quietly to herself. So much for staying in the moment.

Zach took a moment to take in the sunset. He couldn't remember the last time he had slowed down to do something so basic. He also couldn't remember the last time a woman had gotten under his skin like Bridget had. Considering his upbringing and life experiences, he had kept his heart guarded.

And he never crossed the line when it came to work and his personal life.

You're officially on leave, remember? No lines crossed.

He filled his lungs, then slowly exhaled. Sounded like an excuse to him.

The kiss had been innocent, but perhaps he had been selfish. Maybe a little curious, too. Bridget had enough on her mind without him playing with her emotions. Yet he couldn't help himself. She looked so pretty, the sun catching the gold specks in her hair, the sunset casting her in the perfect light.

He took a step backward and rubbed the back of his head. Yeah, he probably should have resisted the impulse to kiss Bridget. His life didn't leave room for women like her. Someone who'd eventually want a husband and kids. A normal life. His life, his work, were anything but normal. He shook away the thought, realizing the simple kiss, after knowing Bridget for exactly four days, had sent his mind spinning.

Yeah, he definitely needed that leave. He was losing his focus.

Zach squared his shoulders, and after a quick knock on the door of Bridget's grandfather's house, he slipped inside. He found Jeremiah sitting at the table, chewing on the mouthpiece of his pipe, studying something in front of him.

"I suggest you get a good night's sleep." Jeremiah rested his pipe in a tray and turned to look at him expectantly. "We have a lot of work in the morning."

"I think there's been a misunderstanding," Zach said, pausing on the way to the small room off the kitchen where he had slept last night. He wanted to make sure he didn't leave anything behind.

"Oh?" Jeremiah's pale, bushy eyebrow drew down.

"I'm afraid I'm headed back to Buffalo tonight." In that moment, Zach felt sad to be going. For the short time he had been here, he had enjoyed the elderly man's company. By all accounts, he was a faithful follower of the ways of the Amish, but it seemed that age had softened him and allowed him to be more open to the possibilities of the world beyond this small farm.

"And you're taking Bridget?" He folded the small paper and tucked it under a black leather-bound book. Without waiting for an answer, he added, "We'll be sad to see her go." He pushed back from the table, and the smooth, carved pine legs on the chair screeched on the hardwood floor.

"Bridget is staying," Zach said, wanting to deliver some good news to this kindly old man.

"For how long?"

"I don't know." Mentally Zach sifted through all the information, but before he could say more, Jeremiah held up a shaky hand, gnarled from years of hard labor. "We still have to—"

"I don't want to know."

Zach laughed, imagining the list of chores Jeremiah had in mind. "I appreciate your hospitality, thank you."

Jeremiah seemed to consider this. He adjusted his glasses on his face. "Ah, yeah, I suppose I shouldn't have looked a gift horse in the mouth."

"Well..." Zach started to say goodbye when the elderly man grabbed his cane resting against the table and slowly walked toward him.

"I don't need to know what's going on in the outside world, but I can see what's going on right outside my home." He gestured to the view from the window over the small kitchen table.

Zach reflected on his tender interaction with Bridget moments ago. Perhaps her grandfather had been watching them, misinterpreting it. *Is he?* He opened his mouth to explain, then snapped it shut. There was nothing to explain.

Jeremiah dragged his hand through his beard in a contemplative manner. "You got family?"

Zach shrugged, a nonanswer, then realized Bridget's grandfather would never accept that. "My mom lives in Buffalo. I don't see much of her."

Jeremiah tilted his head. "Why is that?"

"Long story."

"I've got plenty of time." Jeremiah pinned Zach with a steady gaze. "Family is important. That's something the Amish got right." He raised his hand, palm up. "I have this cozy little house right on the property. My family takes care of me."

"Can't say my family is the same. We're what people might call dysfunctional." Zach hadn't planned to get into any details with this chatty old man.

"I can tell you're hurt. The hurt doesn't go away if you keep feeding it."

Zach tossed another brick on the wall he had built around his heart. "You don't know my mother."

"Forgiveness is not only for those who are receiving it." Jeremiah motioned to nothing in particular with his chin. "You need to let go of the hurt."

"I'll take that under advisement." Zach carefully chose his words. He didn't want to offend Bridget's grandfather. His mother didn't deserve forgiveness. People who made choices like she had would never change.

"Before you go, I could use some help." Jeremiah shuffled over to him. "We're expecting heavy rain in a few days, and I need to clean out the gutters."

Zach tilted his head and smiled. "You want me to clean your gutters? I was going to hit the road tonight."

"Can you make time for an old man? I was thinking we'd get started first thing in the morning." Jeremiah waved his hand and made his final plea, "They're not going to clean themselves."

Zach bit back a sigh and agreed.

The next morning, a commotion sounded outside her childhood home. Bridget sprang out of bed. She planted her hands on the sill and strained to listen.

"Go on now." Bridget's grandfather was talking to someone outside her line of sight.

Bridget spun back around. Liddie's bed had already been made. A pang of guilt jolted her. If she planned on staying—for the week, at least—she should help with chores. Make an effort. Stop treating her parents' home like a bed-and-breakfast.

Bridget hurriedly washed her face and got ready for the day, making sure her hair was neatly tucked under her bonnet. She paused when she caught her reflection in the mirror and stared at her *kapp* and makeup-free face. How was it possible to look so much like the young woman who had escaped in the middle of the night at age twenty, but to feel like a completely different person inside? Wasn't she a different person?

A wave of certainty stiffened Bridget's spine. She could play the role for a few days. Whatever it took to remain safe. She went downstairs. Her mother was sitting at the kitchen table doing some mending. "Hello, sleepyhead."

Bridget drew up short. "What time is it?"

"I'll be getting lunch ready soon."

"Oh… I had no idea." Bridget must have been exhausted. "If you don't mind, I'm going to take a walk. I'll come back in time to help you with lunch."

"Of course," her mother said. She gave her daughter an expression that Bridget couldn't quite read.

"Thirty minutes okay?"

"Perfect."

Bridget nodded and stepped outside. A soft late-morning breeze kicked up the hem of her dress. She stepped off the porch and went in search of her grandfather. She found him around the side of his house giving instructions to a man on a ladder. A man who looked most definitely like Special Agent Zach Bryant dressed in plain clothing with a straw hat perched on his head. She blinked a few times, feeling a smile pull on her lips. He was the most handsome "Amish" man she had ever seen.

Shielding her eyes with her hand, she looked up at

Zach at the top of the ladder. "I thought you were going to leave?"

Zach cut his eyes toward her grandfather. "Me too." A handsome smile lit his face. "Your grandfather is persuasive." He reached into the gutter with a gloved hand and pulled out a stack of leaves and threatened to drop them on Bridget's head.

She took a giant leap back and laughed. "You wouldn't."

"Then you better stay out of my way. I've got work to do here."

The sweet country air filled Bridget's lungs. One of her brothers ran toward the *dawdy haus* with the wheelbarrow, and the other one had a rake. In their plain clothing and straw hats, one brother was hard to distinguish from the other. Caleb and Elijah were both growing into strong young men. Bridget hated the idea of not being a part of their lives once she left again. She quickly shoved the idea away and focused on this very moment. *Be present.*

Her grandfather was in his element, giving directions to those under his charge. Liddie appeared after a while and then disappeared, promising to return with sandwiches. She waved Bridget off when she offered to come in and help. The only element that created a whiff of tension was when their father crossed the yard on the way from the barn to the house. His silent disdain was palpable.

Shortly after Zach finished clearing the gutters and her brothers pushed the wheelbarrow into the line of trees and dumped the leaves, her sister emerged with sandwiches and sliced apples. She spread out a large tablecloth over the picnic table. Liddie encouraged Bridget to join her family for the meal despite the *Bann*. "No one out here is going to mind. Please sit," Liddie whispered. "Besides, Zach's not exactly on the path to Amish baptism." Liddie laughed at her own joke, and their grandfather shook his head, light dancing in his eyes.

"My friend Zach was good enough to dress the part," Jeremiah said. "I figured it might appease your father." Her grandfather added the last little bit in a tone that suggested there was no appeasing her father.

Bridget found her gaze drifting toward the house. She suspected her father was watching them. She could sense his disapproving gaze. She shook off the foreboding feeling. She owed her father respect, but she was an adult and had to make her own decisions. She refused to give up her calling for him.

Bridget took a seat next to Zach. She closed her eyes briefly, then opened them, half expecting that the family that surrounded her—and this handsome man who had come suddenly into her life—would be gone.

They weren't. They were right here. With her. Under the warm summer sun.

Bridget took a bite of her sandwich and savored it. All of it.

Because soon, this would all be gone.

TWELVE

Bridget ran her thumb over the flat surface of a perfect skimming rock while Zach took a phone call on their after-lunch stroll. She walked a little bit ahead to give him privacy. She palmed the rock, gauging its weight. Being out here brought back carefree memories from her childhood when she and her siblings had finished their chores and then escaped to the pond. She tossed up the rock and caught it in the same hand, then zinged it across the pond.

One. Two. Three. Four. She counted the skips before the rock sank to the water's depths.

An exceptionally good skipping rock combined with the right flick of the wrist had her looking around to share her excitement. She found Zach watching her, a smile softening the hard plains of his face. "Nice." Zach flashed her a thumbs up, then checked the phone again. He had graciously agreed to go for a walk with her when she knew his plans to return to Buffalo had already been derailed multiple times. And based on the phone calls, he probably couldn't delay his return much longer.

The knot of dread in her stomach had loosened a fraction, replaced by something she was afraid to identify. She hadn't felt this kind of spark since Moses Lapp had courted her. No, not even then. Moses had been more persistent in pursuing her than she had been in being pursued. She had accepted the rides and his attention because Bridget thought maybe if she found the right partner, she'd finally settle in and do what was expected of her. Be the nice Amish girl.

Obviously, it hadn't taken.

"You're pretty good at that," Zach said, stuffing his cell phone into the back pocket of his jeans.

"I've had a lot of practice." She forced a nonchalance into her tone. She gestured toward the phone with her chin. "Sounded important." She'd never get used to how cell phones had the potential to interrupt any of life's moments. Part of her didn't want Zach to tell her what the call was about so they could continue their outing and shut out the world for a little bit longer.

Bridget bent down and picked up another rock, then dropped it. She rubbed her hands together to get rid of the grit.

"I have some bad news," Zach finally said. She closed her eyes briefly, wanted to stop this conversation, stop it from happening here where she had so many happy memories.

Bridget crossed her arms tightly over her chest to brace herself. *Please, dear Lord*, she prayed, not knowing what she was pleading for.

"Dr. Ryan's dead."

Bridget's arms fell, and she rocked back on the heels of her boots. The news set every inch of her skin on fire. "Dr. Ryan? He was in jail."

Zach took a step closer to her. He seemed hesitant before lifting his hand and gently cupping her elbow. "Someone got to him."

A wave of nausea rolled over her. "Someone got to him?" she repeated, trying to figure out how that had happened. Her pulse chugged in her ears, making her feel disoriented. "How is that possible in jail?"

"I wish I could say it's impossible. It's not. People can be paid off." Zach scrubbed a hand across his face.

"His poor family." Tears burned the backs of her eyes. "His poor wife." She shook her head slowly, feeling sick. "His sons."

"The doctor didn't deserve to die. No one does. Not like that."

Bridget lifted her eyes to study his. "I started all of this…" A warm breeze fluttered her dress and made her shudder.

"You didn't start this." He pulled her close and wrapped his arms around her. "This is not your fault."

She stepped back, out of his embrace, suddenly in a panic. "I shouldn't have come here. I've put my family in danger." *You knew that all along. You never think. You're selfish.* The voice of self-doubt mocked her. "I can't stay here anymore."

Zach caught her hand and stopped her frantic movements. "You are safe here. You have not put your family in danger. You've done everything right. You came forward when you suspected Dr. Ryan. You did the right thing," he repeated. "These drugs are killing people."

The intensity of his last statement made her blood run cold. She locked gazes with his probing brown eyes. "Your sister's death has given your life purpose."

He never took his eyes off her. "I can't go back in time and bring my sister back. But I can save other people from suffering the same fate." He dragged a hand through his hair. He bent and picked up a rock, dropped it, then found another. He flung it, and the stone sank fast and deep.

His vulnerability drew her closer. "My father warned

me—warned all of us about the dangers of the outside world. I never wanted to listen."

"Do you really think nothing bad can go on here?"

"Not like in Buffalo." Bridget slipped her arm around his back and placed her head on his strong shoulder. What if they had met under different circumstances? What if he didn't live his life undercover?

Zach kissed the top of her head. "I never should have left my sister. Leann got involved with the wrong people, and my mother was helpless to stop it." His solid chest rose and fell on a heavy sigh. "For all I know, my mom was the one who brought the drug dealers into my sister's life. I should have stayed and gotten the both of us out of there."

Bridget looked up at him, his face only inches from hers. She resisted the urge to reach up and run the tips of her fingers across the stubble of his unshaven jaw. He looked good. He always looked good, but she preferred him clean-shaven. Maybe because all the men in her life growing up had beards. A clean-shaven man represented the outside world to her. "Maybe you should go see her."

"No point." Zach smiled sadly. "I can't forgive her. She'll never change."

Bridget shifted her gaze to the pond, not quite ready to step away from Zach. Tiny diamonds of sunlight danced on the pond's small ripples in the soft breeze. "Forgiveness isn't only about the other person. It's about finding peace in your heart. If you forgive your mom for what you suspect are her shortcomings—"

"Suspect?" He interrupted, the single word sharp and accusatory. He stepped away from her. "I know what my mother was like."

"Okay," Bridget said softly, "okay. If you can forgive your mother for not being the mother she needed to be, it doesn't mean you accept what she did or didn't do. It means you've forgiven her shortfalls and can move forward in your own life without the burden."

"Your grandfather was talking about forgiveness, too," Zach grumbled. "Well, that might not work in the real world."

"This is no less the real world than life in Buffalo. My family and my ancestors chose to live this way. Separate from the world. And considering everything that's going on in the outside world, it's not necessarily a bad choice." The weight of her message had her lowering herself onto a large rock and stretching her legs out in front of her. "This whole situation with Dr. Ryan and the drugs is never going to go away for me, is it?" She adjusted her long skirt over her legs and studied her boots. "I'm never going to be safe if I go back to Buffalo."

His concerned look said more than any words could.

"Maybe this is a giant sign." Bridget held up her palms to the sky.

"A sign that, what, you're supposed to move back to Hickory Lane?" Zach took a step back and held out his arms. She had definitely hit a sore spot.

Bridget dropped her hands into her lap. "Yes. It's like God wanted to show me how truly dangerous the outside world was. That I should have never left the Amish. It was selfish of me to only consider my own wants." All the thoughts that had been swirling around her head came pouring out.

Zach drew closer and crouched down next to Bridget, clasping his hands between his knees. "I'm not the best person to be talking about God and what He wants. I'm not willing to consider this forgiveness angle you're trying to sell—" he laughed, a mirthless sound "—but I believe those who choose to go into nursing are hardly the selfish sort."

Bridget lifted her gaze to meet his. "It's hard to feel like I'm doing the right thing when my entire world is imploding." She dragged her pinched fingers down the length of the string on her bonnet. "Maybe my life would be less complicated if I stayed here." Was she just looking for someone to tell her what to do?

He gently tapped the back of her hand with his clasped hands. "Do you really believe that? Would you be happy?"

Bridget pressed her lips tighter. "Life is not about happiness. It's about being selfless. About caring for others."

"You've described nursing," Zach said, his voice gravelly, like the small pebbles sliding under the heels of her boot.

"I've missed my family." Sitting here by the pond, she could almost see her younger brothers horsing around, skimming rocks. Proclaiming themselves to be the winner. A hollowness expanded in her chest. "Until I walked into the coffee shop and met you, I hadn't taken more than a minute to look up from my books. Now that that's all been stripped from me, I realize I have nothing else."

"You have me." The openness on his face suggested he was baring his soul.

It was Bridget's turn to smile sadly. "I don't have you." Her pulse beat wildly, making her own words sound faraway in her ears. She flinched, as if the notion was ridiculous. "Besides," she quickly backtracked, "you'll soon go on to another case. Your life is undercover. Pretending to be someone else."

Zach jerked back, almost losing his balance in his crouched position. He straightened and looked out toward the water, then he looked back at her. "Is that what you think I've been doing? Pretending?"

Bridget lowered her head, heat stinging her cheeks. "We've known each other for less than a week. None of this can be real."

Zach and Bridget walked back to the farm in silence. Her stinging words gave him pause. Were his feelings a product of everything they both had been through? Her carefully crafted world had suddenly spun out of control, and his all-or-nothing undercover assignments had sent him on a path of self-destruction a long time ago. He hadn't been real with himself—with anyone—for a very long time. It took practice to suppress who you really were to pretend to be someone else when you were undercover. No one said he wasn't good at his job.

Probably too good.

Had he reached for Bridget because he was drowning? Needed a lifeline? Wanted to know what it would be like to be a part of someone's life? Someone who was so genuine. So real. But how was that fair to her?

"I thought maybe you fell in," Bridget's grandfather joked when they got back.

"No, I was enjoying the pond. I've missed this place." There was a wistful quality to her voice that made Zach wonder if she were truly considering staying.

"I got seven skips the other day," Caleb joined in enthusiastically. He and his grandfather were the only two still sitting by the picnic table.

"You must have taken lessons from your sister," Zach said.

Bridget's eyes widened a fraction, recognizing his compliment was meant to break the dark mood surrounding them ever since their heart-to-heart discussion.

"No way," Caleb replied, oblivious to the exchange

between Zach and Bridget. "I taught her everything she knows."

"He did." Bridget gently patted her brother's cheek, seemingly lost in thought.

"Well," Zach said, "I better hit the road before Jeremiah assigns me any more chores." He turned to the elderly man. "Thanks for putting me up."

"I appreciated your help today," Jeremiah said, running a hand down his beard. "It's been a few years since I've been able to climb a ladder."

"No problem," Zach said. He enjoyed the simplicity of the tasks and a job completed without any complications.

"I better see if Liddie needs any help in the kitchen," Bridget suddenly blurted out. Splotches of pink blossomed on her cheeks. "If I'm going to be staying here, I need to pull my weight." She clapped her hands together and bowed her head slightly. "Thanks for everything. I trust you'll keep me apprised of…" she seemed to be searching for the right word "…everything."

"Sure." Zach hated how awkward everything suddenly felt. Before he had a chance to smooth things over, she spun around and jogged toward the house.

"Why don't you go help your sister, Caleb?" Jeremiah suggested.

"In the kitchen?" He seemed horrified.

"Or I could find more gutters for you." Jeremiah gave his grandson a pointed stare.

"All right…" The boy's shoulders sagged, and he ran after his sister.

"I'm going to change and then head out." Zach slipped into the *dawdy haus* and a few minutes later returned to find Jeremiah waiting for him.

"It wonders me why you're so quick to leave," Jeremiah said.

"There's been a development."

"Oh." The older gentleman seemed to consider this for a moment. "I hope this means my granddaughter will be safe."

"I'll make sure she's safe, sir."

"Seems like a hard thing to do if you're in Buffalo and she's in Hickory Lane."

The screen door slammed, and Caleb ran outside, followed by Elijah. The older brother grabbed a volleyball and lobbed it over the net set up on the far side of the property.

"She's safe here," Zach said.

Jeremiah made a noncommittal sound. "Bridget's a lot like me. Not sure she knows it. I don't talk much about my youth. She's got a restless spirit." He stared off into the middle distance, considering something, then he snapped his attention back to Zach. "She's a good kid, and she needs to follow her own path."

"Yes, I've come to see that in the short time that I've known her." Zach swatted at a mosquito that landed on the back of his hand.

Jeremiah waved a weathered hand. "When this situation is under control, you need to convince Bridget to go back to school. Become a nurse."

Zach glanced back at the house, then at Jeremiah. "That's not my job." He wasn't sure she'd appreciate his interference anyway, especially if she didn't believe it was genuine. Had he truly lost sight of himself with all the years of being undercover?

"Did your job require that you clean out my gutters?"

Zach laughed. Nothing got past Jeremiah Smucker. The screen door creaked open again, and Bridget appeared, drying her hands on her apron. She lingered a moment, then slipped back inside.

Jeremiah limped toward his little house. "Come in for some tea."

Zach hated to refuse the kindly old man. "Don't mind if I do."

The two men settled in at the small kitchen table. Jeremiah was the first to speak. "When I was a little younger than Bridget, I left Hickory Lane. Made it all the way to Wyoming. Worked on a ranch for two years. It was beautiful country. Mountains. Landscape like I've never seen."

"Why'd you come back?"

"Word got to me that my father died, and my mother wasn't well enough to take care of the farm. Since I was the oldest, my siblings were looking to me to help." He patted his thigh. "I had saved up a tidy sum working on the ranch. I came back and saved the farm, as they say. Started courting my Sarah…" He held out his hand in a sweeping gesture. "And here we are."

Through the window, the men watched the young Miller boys by the volleyball court. Caleb spent more time chasing the ball than lobbing it over the net. Elijah shifted his weight from foot to foot in frustration or boredom, maybe a little of both.

"I'm happy I came back. This is where I was meant to be."

"I don't understand." Zach took a sip of his tea, then set his mug back down. "You're happy here. Why are you asking me to convince Bridget to leave?"

"Bridget is meant to be a nurse. She won't be content here."

Zach nodded. "Okay… I'll do what I can once it's safe for her to come home." He didn't know what else to say. "Does Bridget know about your adventures?"

"Neh." Jeremiah palmed his pipe. "It's something best not discussed. I need to lead by example. You understand."

Zach nodded.

Seemingly satisfied, Jeremiah scooted away from the table and returned with two pieces of pie. "Figured you'd like something sweet."

Zach picked up his fork. "Looks great." The two men ate and chatted like old friends. After a while, Zach asked, "Do you ever wonder about the life not lived?" Zach often wondered that himself. How different would things be for him, his sister, his mother. Drugs had infiltrated the lives of all those he loved and changed them irrevocably. His poor, sweet sister had died of an overdose, and he spent a life pretending he was someone he wasn't to catch drug dealers.

"There's no sense in doing that at my age. I've had a good life. *Gott* had a plan. He's blessed me with a wonderful family. I wouldn't change a thing." He smooshed a few crumbs that had fallen on the table with his finger, then dropped them on his plate. "I might have to deny this if you share what I'm about to say with the bishop. The Amish are a good people. A godly people. But I know in my heart that there are good, *Gott*-fearing people out there." He lifted his hand, indicating the general "out there." He smiled slowly. A wariness lingered in his eyes. "I love Bridget. I'd love her to stay in Hickory Lane, but I feel *Gott* has called her to be a nurse so she can help people." He looked at Zach expectantly. "Did she tell you how she decided she wanted to be a nurse?"

"Yes."

"Well, then you know how important it is." He nodded his head slowly. "If it's within your power, make sure Bridget doesn't give up on that dream."

"Not sure I have that kind of power."

"I've seen you with her."

Zach wanted to protest, but this man didn't miss much.

"You care about her," Jeremiah added.

"I do," Zach admitted. "She's an incredible woman." He frowned. "I'm afraid our careers are going to take us in completely different directions."

"They don't have to." Jeremiah's matter-of-fact tone gave Zach pause.

Zach slowly pushed back from the table, feeling uncomfortable at the turn of the conversation. "It's getting late."

"You're good company."

"So are you." Zach smiled. He genuinely liked Bridget's grandfather. He'd miss him when this was all over.

"But you're not very smart."

Zach laughed. "I'm afraid to ask."

Jeremiah reached for his cane propped up near the table. He made no effort to stand. "There's an old Amish saying, 'A man is never old until his regrets outnumber his dreams.'"

I must be very, very old. Zach kept the thought to himself. No sense spoiling a great day.

THIRTEEN

When Bridget first wandered outside on the porch, she hadn't realized Zach was still there. When she saw him chatting with her grandfather, she found herself doing an about-face and slipped back inside. The mention of her name made her pause at the screen door. She hadn't meant to eavesdrop. Her grandfather didn't exactly have what she heard some of her fellow nursing students call an indoor voice.

"When this situation is under control, you need to convince Bridget to go back to school. Become a nurse." A wave of heat washed over her. Her grandfather's request baffled her. Zach had no authority over her. Why would he ask that of him? Didn't her grandfather want her to be baptized and stay in Hickory Lane?

Later, while Bridget was reading on the back porch, she was surprised to see Zach just then leaving the *dawdy haus*. Bridget tossed her book aside and strode across the yard to meet the DEA agent who had come into her life only recently and turned everything upside down. Or, more fairly, her life had been turned upside down not coincidentally at the same time she met him.

"Hi." His brown eyes seemed to warm at her presence.

"Hi. You're all set?" Bridget asked, suddenly feeling foolish because they had already said their goodbyes.

Zach patted his bag. "Yes, all set." His eyes twitched a fraction. "You want to walk over to my truck with me?"

Bridget glanced over her shoulder at her parents' house, feeling like she needed permission, even though that was ridiculous. "Sure. You and my grandfather had a long visit."

"He's a nice man."

"He is."

They crossed the field in silence; flecks of mud splashed up on her boots. The words she really needed to say clung to the back of her throat, making each second feel precious. Finally, when they stepped onto the neighbor's gravel driveway, where Zach's truck was parked, she turned to face him. "I feel like I put my foot in my mouth by the pond. I'm sorry. I shouldn't have said what I said. I had no right." Now that she'd found the words, they spilled out. "Thank you for everything you've done."

"It's my job." He popped open the tailgate and tossed his duffel bag under the tonneau cover. He must have sensed her mood, because he turned and said, "We're going to figure this out. You're going to be able to come back to Buffalo and finish school."

There it is.

Bridget glanced down at her boots, then up at him. "I heard part of your conversation with my grandfather. Your voices carried across the yard and through the screen door." Her face flushed hot again. "It's not your job to make sure I pursue my dream. I don't want that weight on you. I made my own choices when…well, from the time I first sat down at Dr. Ryan's computer. I could have looked the other way. My job was nearing its end. I could have gone back to school quietly. It would have been so much easier," she muttered. Her stomach knotted at the reality of it all. "I made my own choices, and I'll work through the consequences."

Zach reached out and brushed a strand of hair away from her face. Her skin singed under his touch. "I'm not going to abandon you. I'm going to put whoever's involved in this in jail and make sure you're free to do whatever you want in life." A small smile flashed on his lips. He seemed to hesitate a moment, then took a step back.

Bridget took a step forward. She planted her hand on his chest and leaned up on her tiptoes. They locked eyes for the briefest of moments before she leaned in and kissed him. He wrapped both his arms around her and pulled her close. She grew more confident from his strength.

Reluctantly, she broke off the kiss. "I wanted to let you know that I didn't think you were pretending. I'm not pretending, either. I really like you, but we both know life is pulling us in different directions." She reached behind her and removed his arm and stepped out of his embrace.

"Hey," he said, his voice husky. "I am going to do everything in my power to make sure you get back to school. Become a nurse."

Bridget looked up at him and squinted against the late-afternoon sun, its beams diffused through the nearby trees. "I'm not your responsibility." *Like your sister wasn't.*

"I care about you..." Zach took a step closer and cupped her cheek. This time she didn't back away. She took a step closer, and he kissed her gently on the lips. She rested her head on his solid chest. If only they had met under different circumstances. He pressed her close to him. A door opening sounded close by. The neighbors.

Bridget stepped back, a twinge of embarrassment snaking its way through the momentary feelings of warmth, connection.

"Let me drive you home," he said.

Bridget shook her head. "It's only across the field." She smiled. "I'm safe here."

Bridget watched him climb into his truck, then she turned to stroll across the field, wondering if she'd ever feel as safe as she had in his arms.

The entire drive back to Buffalo, Zach couldn't get the thought of Bridget's soft lips out of his mind. His last memory of her was her long dress blowing in the wind and her shielding her eyes from the sun before she turned to cut across the field to go home. He had no business getting involved with someone who was part of his investigation. *Technically, you're on leave.* That argument didn't squash his concern that she was Amish. They could never be together. No, she wasn't Amish. She was hiding among the Amish.

He rubbed the back of his neck, wishing he could clear his head. Figure this out.

The kiss had been innocent. Yet he had never crossed the line while working on a case. Hadn't he? *Well, never romantically.* Bridget was straddling two worlds; he could read the indecision in her eyes. And his work was his world. One undercover case after another. He had created a life where having a family was next to impossible. He laughed to himself. The two of them made a pair, both trying to figure out where they fit in the world.

Zach had spent most of his life pretending he was someone he wasn't: a dealer, a junkie in need of a fix, the lookout. A guy could get lost in all the pretending. Bridget hadn't been wrong in suggesting he was good at it.

He wasn't pretending with her.

The green-and-white Thruway signs announcing the first few Buffalo exits came into view. He scrubbed his

hand across his face when he saw the familiar sign announcing the exit to his childhood neighborhood. He lived
in Buffalo, but he rarely drove the same streets he used to
travel on his first ten-speed bike.

As if the truck had a mind of its own, Zach found himself merging off the highway. It was getting late, so he decided he'd drive by his mother's house. He wouldn't stop.
Maybe.

He passed the ice cream stand—a long line snaked in
front of a single order window—the same one that he and
his little sister used to ride their bikes to and buy cones
from with the money he made cutting grass. He shoved
aside the thought and almost turned back before he decided to push through, despite the feelings of nostalgia.

Zach slowed as he drove down his tree-lined childhood
street. Each tree and house were so familiar he could tell
which trees had died or been cut back since his days of
playing hide-and-seek in the neighborhood. All the shades
on the windows on the Meadows's house were drawn.
Maybe they were all at Ashley's wake?

Too much death in his line of business.

His childhood home hunkered in the gathering shadows.
He pulled over along the curb. With his bent arm resting
on the open window frame, he sat in silence, trying to remember the kid he had once been. Despite the five-year
age gap, he and his little sister had been close. Very close.
In one of his psychology classes in college, he'd learned
that kids of dysfunctional parents tended to lean on one
another because that's all they had. He didn't need to take
a three-credit college-level class to learn that. He lived it.

His attention drifted to the small detached garage. The
shadow of the basketball net brought him back to their spir-
ited games of H-O-R-S-E. Leann loved that game. He was
about to write this off as a very bad idea when the distinct

scent of cigarette smoke reached his nose. The sickening, sweet scent of his mother's brand. Then he saw it. The orange glow grew brighter.

"Aren't you going to say hello?" Her raspy voice floated across the yard.

Zach closed his eyes momentarily to gather himself. He unclicked his seat belt and climbed out. He crossed the yard. He hadn't been here since the day of Leann's funeral.

He walked up to the porch and stuffed his hands in his jean pockets. "Hi, Mom." The word sounded foreign on his lips.

"Zachary." She said his name reverently, then stiffened. "Are you in the neighborhood because of Ashley?" He felt his mother's watchful gaze from the shadows.

"This whole case got me thinking about home," he admitted.

The tip of her cigarette glowed orange again. She released a billow of smoke between thin lips. "Least something got you back here." A strangled laugh-cough took him right back to his youth.

Zach climbed the steps and remembered posing here in his tux before prom. He leaned back against the railing, facing his mom, his eyes adjusting to the dusk. "I've been busy."

His mother had aged. Life hadn't been kind to her. He had expected her to be itching for a fight. Man, she loved a good fight. He held his breath. Her face softened, and she ran the back of her cigarette hand across her cheek. "I don't blame you for not coming around." She cleared her throat. "How have you been?"

"I'm okay. Work's busy." His mom had laughed when he signed on with the DEA, suggesting the work was a bit on the nose. "Lots of drugs in the world."

"Was Ashley into drugs?" His mother looked out over

the yard in a thousand-mile stare. "Is that how she ended up murdered?"

"No. By all accounts, Ashley was a good kid. Wrong place, wrong time."

"She came here looking for you. Maybe if I hadn't given her your card." His mother's voice cracked for the first time.

"Not your fault, Mom," Zach said, his heart softening toward the only family he had left.

A soft laugh escaped her lips. "I better have my hearing checked. I never could do anything right in your mind."

His mother had gotten lost in her struggle with addiction. So had her daughter. And if he was being honest, he had, too. He had become single-minded in his focus. So judgmental.

Unforgiving.

His brief time in Hickory Lane had had a profound impact on him.

"How have you been doing, Mom?"

"Still working at the garden center." She had lost her nursing license years ago. She stubbed out her cigarette on the ashtray next to her chair. "I've been sober three years now."

Three years!

"That's great." Zach leaned back and wrapped his hands around the railing. He hated how formal they sounded.

"Yeah, I'm proud of myself." She stood and approached him. She placed the palm of her hand on his cheek. "My baby boy."

Emotion welled up in his throat, making it impossible to speak. The familiar scent of her shampoo mingled with the tobacco still lingering in the air.

"Do you have anyone special?" She tilted her head, curiosity lighting her eyes. "Sure you do. Look at you."

"There's someone," he found himself saying. "But my job makes it hard."

His mother's lips pinched. "Don't put anything above a loved one. Not anything."

Zach made a noncommittal sound. *A loved one?* It seemed too early to put Bridget in that category.

She dropped her hand and inhaled deeply. "You are one of the few things I did right."

Zach forced an awkward smile. After a moment, he found his voice. "I know you did your best."

His mother tucked in her chin, then looked up at him. Tears shone in her eyes. "You and your sister deserved more. I wish I had been able to give it to you. To both of you." Her regret was palpable.

"You need to forgive yourself."

His mother dipped her head.

The next words he had to force through the emotion clogging his throat. "I forgive you. You're human. We all make mistakes."

His mother gripped the gold pendant hanging around her neck, and a single tear tracked own her cheek.

Zach tapped his palm on the railing. "Well, I better go."

His mother took a step back and swatted at what he suspected was a mosquito. "Yes, it's getting buggy out here." She gave him a sad smile. "I'm glad you stopped by, Zachary. Maybe you'll come back again soon. When you have more time."

"Yeah…" He descended the steps.

"Maybe you can bring your friend," she added hopefully.

"Maybe." He climbed into his truck and slammed the door. A myriad of emotions played at his heartstrings. Lightness. Relief. Hope. Maybe there was something to be said about this forgiveness stuff.

FOURTEEN

A crack of thunder startled Bridget awake. She pulled the quilt up to her ear, wishing she could drift back to sleep in her childhood bed. She had been up late many nights over the past two weeks. She and Zach had gotten into a routine of catching up late in the evening. She'd tuck her cell phone between her shoulder and ear and let his deep voice wash over her while she rocked slowly in one of the back porch chairs. It was her favorite time of day.

Fortunately, she found a way to charge her phone and laptop by using her grandfather's generator that conveniently had the right outlet. Bridget believed he secretly enjoyed helping her stay in touch with Zach despite his half-hearted reminders that she was breaking the rules. Seemed to take one rule breaker to facilitate another one.

During their conversations, she and Zach shared everything from the details about her quiet days on the farm to how he was keeping busy by completing long-neglected house projects. There weren't many updates on her case, but he finally opened up to her on why he was on leave from the DEA. He was struggling with his guilt over the death of a young confidential informant. He felt responsible. The CI had taken too many risks. Now his boss worried Zach was on the cusp of burnout and needed to walk away. Albeit temporarily. Which lead to discussions about his plans to return to work next week. Would he be allowed to go undercover? Would he still have time for their phone calls?

On her end, she wondered if she'd ever catch up on her nursing classes that weren't online. She hated to postpone graduation next spring.

And where, exactly, did they think this relationship was going?

Another crash, this time louder, made her bolt upright. She blinked a few times. Heavy rain blurred the view from her second-story bedroom window. Liddie's bed was empty. Farm chores didn't stop for bad weather.

A familiar guilt nudged her. She hadn't exactly been carrying her weight since she'd been back, mostly because she had really hoped that it was going to be a very temporary situation. Sure, she helped her *mem* with dinner and keeping the house, but she had left the farm chores to her siblings and her *dat*. He was the only one actively shunning her, which basically meant he didn't talk to her and she had to eat her dinner on the back porch. Other than that, she had been able to get reacquainted with her family.

Boy, she had missed them. The daily interaction. The laughter.

Deep down, she worried that the longer she stayed in Hickory Lane, the harder it would be to leave again. She tossed the quilt back and quickly got dressed. She scurried downstairs in bare feet and came up short when she found her parents huddled in the kitchen talking in hushed tones. Bridget's blood ran cold.

"What's wrong?" she asked, her voice cracking.

Her mother looked on the verge of tears, and her father stopped speaking. More secrets.

Moving closer, Bridget's heart thudded in her throat.

"Is someone hurt?" Her frantic gaze went to the window, then back to her parents. "Are my brothers okay? Liddie? Please, what's wrong?"

Her mother took a step toward her, twisting a dishrag in her hands. "No one is hurt. Your brothers are in the barn doing their chores."

"Is Liddie with them?" Bridget rushed to the mudroom by the back door and stuffed her feet into one of her boots, the leather cold from the early morning draft swirling in under the back door.

Her father's gaze cut through her. "Liddie's not here." He sounded angry, not distraught, unlike her mother.

Bridget straightened from tying her boot. Icy dread pooled in her gut. "What do you mean?" She wanted to shake her stoic dad. Liddie hadn't mentioned anything about going anywhere. Actually, she'd seemed exceptionally cheery lately. Bridget had thought it was because her big sister had returned.

"It seems…" Her father's cautionary look of warning made her mother's voice trail off.

"You have to tell me," Bridget pleaded.

Her father turned his stony gaze on his oldest daughter. "We don't have to tell you anything. You made your choice to leave this family."

Bridget focused on unclenching her hands, trying to calm her growing frustration. "I know you're mad at me. Stay mad at me. But this isn't about me—it's about Liddie. Why are you upset and where is my sister?"

Her mother sank into one of the kitchen chairs. The oil in the pan on the stove was popping over the flame. Bridget turned off the gas stove and froze, realization slowly creeping in. Her mother was devastated, and her father was his usual stern self.

Rewind the clock five years. Bridget had crept out in

the middle of the night and her sister must have woken up to Bridget's empty bed. Her parents must have huddled in the kitchen, debating what to do. A new wave of guilt slammed into her. Was this how it had been when Bridget disappeared in the middle of the night? Of course, it was. How truly selfish she had been.

What other choice did she have?

Her pulse ticked in her head. She squared her shoulders and asked, "Do either of you have any idea where Liddie might have gone?"

Her mother slowly shook her head. Her ivory skin grew paler. Bridget turned to her father. "*Dat*, any ideas?" She wasn't hopeful. Amish children didn't usually confide in their parents.

Bridget felt her palms sweat.

Why hadn't Liddie confided in her? What if Liddie didn't leave on her own? What if Bridget had brought evil to the peaceful farm? She grew dizzy with the thought.

Bridget toed off her boot and took the stairs two at a time, her long dress flapping around her legs. She tore open the door to the closet and dropped to her knees. She pulled out the folded blanket. Her phone hit the hardwood floor with a resounding *clack*.

She patted the entire blanket, then stretched into the closet and checked the far back corners. Nothing.

She sank back on her heels. A sick wave rolled over her.

Liddie's phone was gone.

Bridget scooped up her phone and checked for reception. Three bars. *Thank You, God.* With shaky fingers, she called Zach. He answered on the first ring.

Zach was lulled out of a fitful sleep by the subtle vibration of his cell phone. He had put it on silent before he collapsed into bed after talking to Bridget late into the night. He feared their budding relationship would complicate his going back to work next week. Well, not if he was stuck behind a desk.

He palmed the offending device and dragged it toward him. He cocked one eye open and looked at the display: Bridget. He pushed up onto an elbow and swiped his finger over the screen. "Hello."

"Zach, sorry to wake you." He could hear the panic in her voice.

"I was up," he said without thinking. "What's wrong?"

"Liddie's gone." Before he had a chance to ask her to clarify, she added, "She wasn't in her bed when I woke up. No one knows where she went. Her cell phone's missing. That must mean she went on her own. That she's not in danger." The last statement sounded more like a question, and he didn't have the answer.

"Did she say anything about leaving?" If she had, Bridget had never mentioned it in their marathon late-night phone calls.

"No." The single word came out in a rush. "I thought we had patched things up a bit and that she would have confided in me." She let out a mirthless laugh. "I never told her I was leaving years ago," she muttered. "I mean, I thought I was protecting her from getting into trouble with our parents or the elders." He could imagine her pained expression. "I'm worried she's doing this to get back at me."

"Don't go there." He pulled clean clothes out of his dresser drawers and headed toward the shower. "I'll help you find her. Any idea where she may have gone?"

"I could contact some of the people who helped me when I left." Her voice grew quiet, as if the phone had moved away from her mouth. "I'm not sure if they have the same phone numbers or if they're still doing that sort of thing."

"Make a few calls. Meanwhile…" He glanced at the digital clock. "I can be there in about an hour."

"Thank you. I'd feel better if we could drive around town and look for her. Maybe she slipped out with friends."

"Sit tight."

Bridget ripped off her bonnet and changed into street clothes. She didn't want to stand out like a sore thumb when Zach picked her up. Liddie may have run off like she had, but Bridget had to make sure.

She bounded back down the stairs and tipped her head to acknowledge her parents and a few of the neighbors gathered in the kitchen. *Already.*

Mrs. Yoder, the grandmother of the child she had saved from choking, sat next to Bridget's mother, no doubt having made the untouched tea sitting in front of them. Her friend's mother smiled softly at Bridget, perhaps forgiving her for any past wrongs.

The atmosphere was downright morose, as if someone had died. Well, for those who left the fold, it was a death of sorts.

Self-consciously Bridget touched her bun. "I'm going out to look for Liddie." An apology for her clothing died on her lips. She loved her parents. She respected their ways. But she wasn't going to keep apologizing for who she was.

Her mother sat at the table with clasped hands. A crease lined her father's forehead, registering his silent disapproval. Bridget ran out the back door and headed toward the barn, sidestepping huge puddles. Thankfully the rain had stopped. Bridget had expected to find her brothers doing their chores. Instead they were sitting on hay bales talking to another young Amish man who had his back to her. She stopped in the doorway at the sound of their voices.

Her brothers seemed unfazed by her *Englisch* clothes. "You heard?" Elijah asked.

"Yah." Bridget wiped her palms on the thighs of her jeans. "Do you know—"

The man twisted to face her. "Hello, Bridget."

She rocked back on her heels and crossed her arms tightly over her chest, suddenly feeling very exposed. "Moses." The boy who had courted her years ago. The boy she might have spent the rest of her life with if she hadn't made a very bold move. "What are you doing here?" Her words came out harsher than she had intended.

Moses gave her a familiar smug look and waited a beat before saying anything, as if he had information that he wasn't quite yet willing to share. Only after she had left him and Hickory Lane did she recognize his behavior for what it was: his way of exerting control. "Nice to see you, too," he finally said. He was still clean-shaven, which meant he hadn't yet married. He was getting a bit long in the tooth. The same could be said of her if she had never left. In the *Englisch* world, however, she was still a baby. Too young to consider marriage. Many of her nursing friends were enjoying dating around. And until Zach, she hadn't given a serious relationship much thought. Education had been her primary focus.

"Do you know where my sister is?" A slow, steady ticking ratcheted up in her head. *What is this really about?*

"Can't say that I do." Moses hopped to his feet and moved toward the barn door. He tipped his hat to Bridget on his way out.

"Wait," Bridget said.

Moses slowed but didn't turn around. She jogged to catch up to him, fury heating her face. "Why are you here?" She didn't believe that he suddenly appeared on her family farm the morning her sister disappeared.

Something flitted across his face. She would have missed it if she hadn't been watching him closely. His eyes widened, as if he were going to make a smart-aleck comment, but instead he said, "Your father came to my family's farm looking for me. He wanted to know if Liddie was with me."

"Why would my sister be with you?" The ticking grew louder.

A slow, smarmy smile tilted his lips. "Didn't she tell you? We've been going together. We weren't doing anything wrong."

So many emotions swirled and expanded in her chest, making it hard to draw a decent breath. "*Neh*, she didn't tell me." Which left her wondering what else her sister hadn't told her. "If you know my sister so well, then where did she go?"

The oily expression slid off his face. "Like I told your father, I don't know. She's been acting strange." He glared at her. "Apparently, you Miller sisters are a lot alike."

"Unless you have something to contribute, I think you should leave." Bridget glared back at him.

"Cool your engines. I was on my way out."

Bridget waited until Moses was gone before she turned to her brothers. "Why did Moses come here?"

Elijah shook his head. "He was trying to find out if we knew where Liddie was. He seemed really mad."

Bridget could only imagine how he had reacted five years ago when he discovered she had left Hickory Lane. Bridget reached out and touched Caleb's arm and asked gently, "Do you have any idea where Liddie is?"

He frowned. "Did she leave us, too?"

Bridget's heart broke. Caleb's face had thinned, lost the roundness of childhood. His eyes mirrored the seven-year-old little boy's that she had abandoned. The little boy she remembered had loved handing her a bouquet of dandelions he had gathered from the field. Tears burned the back of her nose. She swallowed hard. If she owed her preteen brother anything, she owed him the truth. "I don't know. I'll find out."

Elijah jerked his thumb at her jeans. "Are you leaving, too? Or are you dressed to search for our sister?" Hope softened the hard edges of his accusation.

"Right now, I'm looking for Liddie."

"Maybe your police friend can help?" Caleb's voice cracked.

"He's on his way." She tapped Caleb's soft cheek in a rare display of affection. "I love you guys. I won't go anywhere until we know Liddie's safe. I promise."

FIFTEEN

Bridget found her grandfather approaching the barn, his travel hampered by his unsteady footing on the rutted lane.

He pulled his pipe from his mouth. "Is Zach on his way?"

"Yah." Nervous energy made her shift her weight from foot to foot.

"Do you think Liddie would want us to look for her?" He took another long puff on his pipe, regarding her carefully.

"What if…" She couldn't shake the sinking feeling that had been haunting her all morning. "What if she's in danger? What if the people who killed Ashley and Dr. Ryan got Liddie? Maybe they knew where I was and she got in the way somehow."

Liddie took her phone. She probably left on purpose, right? Bridget reasoned to herself. Her gaze drifted to the road, praying that Zach would hurry up and get here.

"Maybe she went on an adventure. Like you," her grandfather said, his tone oddly calm.

Bridget felt a smile pulling at her mouth despite the worry eating away at her. "And like you."

Her grandfather lifted an eyebrow. "You've been talking to someone."

"A lot." She pulled out the pins holding her bun, allowing her hair to drop into a long ponytail. "He only told me about your adventures out west because he thought it would reassure me that I wasn't the only one in the family who had dreams outside Hickory Lane. He didn't mean to betray a confidence. I'm sure of it."

Her grandfather waved his hand. "You're an adult. It's important that you understand your parents and grandparents are people, too. We have lives and dreams outside of our roles in the family."

Bridget had a hard time thinking of her mother and father as anything more than her parents. Especially her father, who was a stickler for rules. She'd never know their true feelings, thoughts, especially if they deviated from the rules of the *Ordnung*. "And sometimes you have to admit there are limits to some relationships."

"I hope whatever you decide to do, you'll send me letters. Keep in touch. Promise?"

Bridget nodded. "Of course." She shoved the tips of her fingers into the back pockets of her jeans. "I'm not going anywhere right now other than to find out where Liddie went. I promise I won't leave without saying goodbye." She had made the same promise to her brother.

Her grandfather laughed. "Liddie's off having fun. I'm sure of it."

Bridget's phone buzzed in her back pocket. She pulled it out and saw a number she didn't recognize. It could be her sister's disposable phone. "Maybe it's Liddie." She quickly swiped her finger across the screen. "Hello."

"Hey, Bridget."

Her heart leaped. "Liddie!"

"Hey, big sis," Liddie said, her voice breaking up over a bad connection.

"Are you okay? Where are you? We're all worried."

The rapid-fire questions allowed no room for answers. "Liddie?"

"I didn't mean to worry you." Wind whistled across the line, yet Bridget still detected a hint of sarcasm. Maybe humor. "Don't tell anyone I called, okay?"

Her grandfather studied her while she talked into the phone. "*Mem* and *Dat* are really worried."

"They'll be fine. It's not like I'm leaving for good."

"Okay, then, where are you?"

Liddie seemed to be muffling the mouthpiece. Was she with someone?

"Tell me where you are," Bridget said again, this time more insistent.

Her sister came back on the line. "Meet us in front of the neighbor's driveway in five minutes. We'll pick you up. And don't tell anyone. If you're not there, we won't stop."

"Liddie…" Bridget dragged out her sister's name, a desperate plea.

"I'm not kidding. You've been where I am. Do this for me." Her little sister. Bridget would do anything for her.

"Who are you—" The call ended abruptly before Bridget had a chance to ask her who she was with or to promise she wouldn't tell anyone. She pulled the phone away from her ear. "Grandpa, that was Liddie. She doesn't want *Mem* or *Dat* to know she called. She's coming to get me." She reached out and touched her grandfather's hand. "I'll bring her home, okay? I called Zach. He's on his way. Keep an eye out for him. Tell him I went to meet Liddie in the neighbor's driveway."

Her grandfather tipped his head; a smile slanted his mouth. "Go on."

"Thanks." Despite the guilt nudging her, she decided against running back inside. "Let *Mem* and *Dat* know that I'll be back after I find Liddie."

He nodded but didn't say anything.

Bridget strode across the field, the shortest distance to the neighbor's house. Phone in hand, she slid her finger across the screen, searching for Zach's contact information. She should probably let him know about the change of plans herself.

"Where are you going?" her father called from the back porch.

She froze, shocked that he was actually speaking to her. She swallowed hard and waved casually. "I'm headed into town. I'm going to see if I can find Liddie."

"You're going to make a mockery of us." Her father glared at her, his gaze running down the length of her *Englisch* clothes.

"I'm sorry, *Dat*. I have to go." Bridget bit back the instinct to reassure her parents that Liddie had called her, that she was okay, but she had promised Liddie. Sort of. She smiled at her mother, who appeared on the porch behind her husband.

A whisper of a smile swept across her mother's face. "Are you leaving for *gut*?"

"Not right now, *Mem*. I'll be back." Bridget's heart broke for her mother. Why did Bridget's dream of becoming a nurse have to come at the expense of her mother's happiness?

"This isn't a bed-and-breakfast," her father called out after her. "You have broken the rules and now your sister thinks she can do the same." He wrapped his work-worn hands around the porch railing, and even from this distance, Bridget sensed his agitation in his fidgety movements.

Of course, her father blamed her.

Bridget's face grew hot.

Suddenly anxious that she'd miss meeting her sister,

she started to jog across the mucky field, wet from the rains last night.

When she reached the bottom of the neighbor's driveway, the sun broke through the dark clouds. Adrenaline hummed through her veins. She turned her focus to the phone again and found Zach's contact information. She was about to call when the deep rumble of an engine vibrated through her. Afraid she didn't have time for a phone conversation before Liddie arrived, she shot Zach a quick text. False alarm. Meeting Liddie now. She's with friend.

Bubbles popped up as if Zach was typing. Bridget glanced up as the loud car roared into view. It was painted an unnatural shade of blue. Something niggled at the base of her brain, sending a cold chill up her spine. Instinctively, she snapped a quick photo of the back end of the car and sent it to Zach. She flicked the switch to silent mode and shoved the phone in her back pocket and tugged her T-shirt over it.

The tinted passenger window whirred down, and her sister's smiling face appeared. She had her hair pulled back in a long ponytail, and she was wearing one of Bridget's T-shirts.

"What are you doing?" Bridget hollered over the loud hum of the engine.

"Of all people, I thought you'd understand." Liddie gave her one of her big, infectious smiles.

Bridget tipped her head to catch a glimpse of the driver. He had on a baseball cap pulled down low. He balanced his wrist on the steering wheel and drummed his fingers to the deep bass of the music. She'd have to hold the questions she had for Liddie until they didn't have an audience.

Liddie tapped her palm on the door frame and craned her neck to look down the road toward the family farm. "Hurry. Get in. Come on—I don't want to be seen."

Bridget hesitated for a fraction of a moment before hopping into the back seat. She slid back and buckled her seat belt. She looked up and met the eyes of the driver in the rearview mirror. A knot tightened in her belly. His shifty gaze returned to the road.

"We need to talk, Liddie," Bridget said.

"I know." Her little sister seemed giddy. "We'll go somewhere. Maybe Jamestown?" She deferred to the driver. "Jamestown cool with you?"

"Sure, no prob," he muttered.

No prob.

That's when it hit her. He was the man who had been sitting by the pool with Liddie in her courtyard back in Buffalo.

"You remember Jimmy, right?" Liddie said cheerfully.

"From my apartment complex." Bridget fought to keep her tone even. "Hi."

Jimmy tipped his head in greeting, but something felt off. Way off.

And his bright blue car. Had it been the same one that nearly ran her over? The incident in the crosswalk had happened so fast that she hadn't remembered the car, but the sound...

She met his gaze in the rearview again, and the hard set of his eyes made her blood run cold. Bridget slipped out her phone and discreetly sent her location to Zach, then slid it under the seat.

Then she said a quick prayer, hoping she was just being paranoid.

Zach was relieved to get the texts from Bridget that Liddie was okay. He tried to keep his eyes on the road, but the phone kept dinging. He glanced down at her last text. It was a photo of a vehicle, its license plate clear. A band tightened around his chest, making it difficult to breath. A metallic blue muscle car. Similar to the one that had nearly run Bridget down in the crosswalk.

Then a strange thing happened. Bridget sent him a link to an app that updated her location in real time. With voice commands, he called her back. "Answer, answer, answer," he muttered aloud to himself. He swerved out into the passing lane, then back into the right lane. When she didn't answer, he shot her a text via voice commands. Don't get in that car. Danger.

His gaze kept drifting to his phone in the cup holder. No response.

The app showed she was moving. He muttered to himself and pounded his fist against the dash. He was at least twenty minutes away. He pressed the accelerator and the mile markers ticked by, but not fast enough.

His phone rang. His ASAC. His heart sunk.

"Hey, boss."

"Hey," Colleen said, her voice crisp and the conversation to the point. "Where are you?"

"I'm on my way to Hickory Lane. I think we have a problem."

"What is it?"

"Bridget just sent me a photo of a car that might be the one that tried to run her down in the crosswalk in Buffalo after she first met with me. I need you to run a plate." His pulse thrummed in his ears. The rearview and side-view mirrors were clear. He changed lanes and passed the snail in front of him.

Come on, come on, come on…

"I can do that. You also need to know that we found video surveillance of a person known to have ties with a street gang entering Dr. Ryan's cell shortly before he was found unresponsive. The video of the attack appears to be missing."

"Why are we just finding this out now?"

"I'm of two minds. The doctor's death is one more case in a heavy caseload. Either it took the officials a while to get around to checking the feed, or someone was paid off to keep the video under wraps."

"Can you send me the video?" The sign ahead indicated his exit was five miles away.

"I'll send a screenshot of his face. It was captured at the jail and they found another image of this guy from the alley behind the clinic."

"Thanks." Then Zach rattled off the license plate from the photo Bridget had sent.

"I'll get back to you on that. One more thing. We've been following the phone records of the gang members. They indicate communication with someone in Hickory Lane. Any chance Bridget has been keeping up with friends back home?"

"I don't think Bridget has any gang friends."

"She's the sort who takes in stray dogs, right? Maybe a person who wormed his way into her life. Maybe she unknowingly compromised her location."

"Not Bridget."

Zach ended the call and pulled up Bridget's GPS location on his phone. She was moving away from Hickory Lane. He got off at the nearest exit and pulled over to study the map closer. He noted the location and entered it into his GPS.

His phone dinged. A grainy photo popped up on his screen. He stared at the image captured on the jail monitors and the security cameras at the clinic. He didn't recognize the man. In the photo from behind the clinic, a second man lurked in the upper right corner. Zach squinted and realization twisted in his gut: this guy was sitting by the pool talking to Bridget's sister right before the Molotov cocktail crashed through the apartment window.

Zach's tires squealed as he pulled away from the curb. Bridget hadn't compromised her location—Liddie had.

SIXTEEN

Sweat pooled under Bridget's arms. Her eyes darted around the back seat. Panic clouded her thinking. Something felt very, very wrong about all this. She could pull the door handle and jump out of the car. Two things gave her pause: the trees whizzing by outside the window and her younger sister in the front seat. She couldn't leave her.

Bridget cleared her throat. "Liddie, we should go back. *Mem* and *Dat* are worried. We can go for a walk around the pond and talk like we used to."

"No, I don't want to go back yet. I want to hang out with Jimmy. You made us leave Buffalo before we got a chance to really get to know each other." Liddie sounded like a petulant child.

"You were going to go home the next day anyway. You didn't miss out on much." Bridget tried to keep her voice even, not let on that she was trying to get away from Jimmy. *Should* she be worried?

There were a lot of bright blue cars, right? Just because Jimmy was in the courtyard prior to the fire in her apartment didn't mean he caused it. Were they in danger or were her instincts off?

"Yeah, we're not going back to the farm." It was then he

took off his baseball cap. Darkness flashed in the depths of his eyes. "And we're not going to Jamestown."

Goose bumps raced across her flesh.

"Where are we going?" Liddie asked, the first hint of apprehension replacing her excitement. Then she squared her shoulders.

"You'll see." Jimmy's tone sounded ominous.

"But I thought…" Liddie let her words trail off.

"Why don't you just take us back home? Our parents are worried." Bridget did her best to keep her voice calm, not wanting to set Jimmy off.

Jimmy laughed and shook his head.

"Take us back home, Jimmy. I changed my mind."

Bridget hated the way her sister was trying to cajole this man into doing the right thing, as if she had to be nice while he ignored her request. Bridget felt sick, fearing the situation was escalating quickly.

When Jimmy responded by pressing on the accelerator, Liddie started pleading in earnest, "Come on, Jimmy, stop. You're scaring me."

Jimmy lashed out, his fist connecting hard and firm with Liddie's cheek. "Shut up!"

Liddie yelped and skittered away, confined by the seat belt. She held her hands to her face.

Hot fury exploded in Bridget's head. "Leave her alone," she growled.

Jimmy laughed again. "You can shut up, too." He pulled out into the passing lane and went around a slower-moving car. "You should have left well enough alone at the clinic," he muttered.

"Why are you doing this? It's over. Dr. Ryan's dead."

"You're joking right?" Disgust dripped from his tone. "You stuck your nose in where it didn't belong. Now you're going to be made an example of." He reached over and dragged his knuckles across Liddie's red check. "If you think of doing something stupid, I'll kill your stupid sister."

Liddie cowered in the passenger seat, making an awful whimpering sound.

What could Bridget do? She already ruled out leaping from the car. And if she tried to distract the punk, they'd go careening into a tree or another car. No, she couldn't risk killing them or some unsuspecting driver.

Bridget stretched her foot and pushed her cell phone deeper under his seat, praying that Zach had gotten her location and was tracking her right now. She was grateful that a coworker had shown her that app, among others, while they ate lunch and chatted.

Jimmy suddenly took a sharp turn and bumped off the road into a field. The jarring turn made Bridget slam her head against the back passenger window. A clattering sound came from under the seat and her phone slid into view, but she couldn't snatch it because she had to brace herself. The car came to an abrupt stop. Liddie groaned.

The second Jimmy put the car into Park, the locks automatically disengaged. Adrenaline propelled Bridget into action. She unclicked her seat belt, snagged her cell phone and pulled the door handle. The door sprang open. She jumped out. The tree line wasn't far. She could make it. Hide.

Get Liddie first.

The whoosh of her pulse roared in her ears.

Bridget's laser-like focus landed on Liddie still sitting in the front seat. Jimmy had her sister's cheeks squeezed between his strong fingers. Her face was contorted in pain. Fear. The glee in his eyes mocked Bridget. He jerked his chin in a cocky gesture as if to say, *Go ahead. Leave. I've got your sister.*

Dear Lord, help us. Help us.

She dug deep, to the depths of her faith, still not seeing how they'd get away from this man. She let out a long, slow breath, and a strange calm washed over her.

Through the windshield she locked gazes with Jimmy. Her shoulders sagged, and she realized they had reached a silent understanding.

Bridget walked over to Liddie's door and opened it, all sense of urgency lost. This wasn't going to be Bridget's escape, but if she complied, it might be Liddie's. Bridget reached in and unbuckled her sister's seat belt while her younger sister quietly sobbed. "It's okay. It's okay. Let's get you out of here."

Liddie looked up at her with a tearstained face. "I'm sorry. I thought he was a nice guy."

"It's okay." She pulled Liddie into a fierce embrace, feeling the time slip away. "I love you."

Liddie sobbed into Bridget's shoulder.

Over her sister's shoulder, Bridget tracked the man as he sauntered around the vehicle. He paused at the rear. The click of the trunk release forced Bridget into action. She didn't have a deal with this man. He was ruthless.

"When I let you go," Bridget whispered in Liddie's ear, "run toward the trees. Run and don't stop. Don't turn around. No matter what."

Liddie stiffened, and Bridget sensed her sister's refusal before she had a chance to voice it. "Now!" Bridget shouted, shocking her sister into action. "Now!" She shoved Liddie toward the tree line, away from the menacing approach of this man.

Liddie tripped. She scrambled to her feet, found her footing and started to run, her forward momentum hampered by the weeds and hidden ruts.

Go, go, go.

Bridget's gaze dropped to Jimmy's hand. *A gun!* Her

knees went to jelly. He lifted the weapon and pointed it at Liddie. A sinister smile tugged on half his mouth. "Should I go for her head or heart?"

Bridget held up her hands, forcing him to focus on her. "It's me you want. Let her go. She's harmless."

He pivoted and aimed the gun at her. She spread out her fingers. "You don't have to do this."

Dear God, please protect me.

"You have no idea what you got yourself into, do you?" He tucked his gun into the back of his pants. His arm snaked out and snatched the phone out of her hand and threw it in the field. He grabbed the front of her T-shirt and twisted and pulled her close. His stale breath reeked of cigarette smoke.

"Please, please, please…" Tears clouded her vision, and panic made her stomach revolt.

Jimmy yanked Bridget forward. She struggled to gain purchase, but he was too strong. Too fast. The tops of her sneakers dragged across the muddy field. The lid of the trunk yawned open, his intent unmistakable.

"Please, please, please, don't do this."

Her hip slammed on the lip of the trunk as he forced her against it. She fought against his hand palming the back of her head. Her feet scrabbled in the mud, a desperate attempt to stop the inevitable.

"Stop struggling," he said, his voice oddly calm. "Ralphie told me not to mess up your face. He wants to make sure I got the right person this time." Had he killed Ashley by mistake? His fingers dug into her neck. The pain made it impossible to think clearly. He positioned her between his hip and the vehicle. He forced her arms behind her and cranked on a zip tie. Bridget's racing mind flashed to Zach doing the same when he arrested the doctor.

Ugh, that hurt.

"Please, don't." Heat swept over her. Knowing this was her last chance, Bridget twisted and flailed. She bent one leg and kneed Jimmy, catching him in the gut. He doubled over in pain. She scrambled forward and lost her balance with her arms fastened behind her back. She fell forward, landing heavily on her shoulder with an oomph.

In a fit of rage, Jimmy grabbed her arm and picked her up handily. He tossed her toward the trunk, and her mid-section slammed on the lip. He forced her the rest of the way in. Her arms were awkwardly bound behind her. His face shook in rage as he hovered over her. He pulled back his fist. "You brought this on yourself."

Gritting his jaw, he punched her in the face like he had done to her sister. Her nose exploded in light and shocking pain unlike anything she had ever experienced. He muttered an expletive and slammed the trunk shut.

Bridget was shrouded in darkness.

All the fight had been beaten out of her.

The engine of Zach's truck purred as he gained on Bridget's location. *Come on, come on, come on.* The indicator on the GPS showing her location had stopped about ten minutes ago. He didn't know if this was good or bad. At the very least, it gave him a chance to catch up.

As he drove beyond Hickory Lane, the occasional farm gave way to fields and trees. "Where are you, Bridget?" he whispered. "Where are you?" The remote location made him pause.

He slowed and double-checked the screen on his cell phone. He had gone past the little blue dot. Zach threw the truck into Reverse, twisted in his seat and rested his forearm on the steering wheel to stare out the passenger window. Trees thick with foliage blocked his view. Still in Reverse, he swerved over to the side of the road and jammed the gear into Park. He jumped out of the truck, keenly aware of the absolute stillness and his gun in its holster.

Why was Bridget's location indicating this field?

An imagine of Kevin Pearson's vacant eyes staring up at him from the empty parking lot flashed in his mind. Zach had had a bead on his location, too. What if he was too late? *Don't go there. Focus.*

With the intensity of an undercover agent going into a stash house, Zach scanned the area. Fresh muddy tire ruts cut into the overgrown vegetation. An image of Bridget sprawled in the field gutted him. He had missed signs that his confidential informant was in danger. He hadn't been there to save his sister. He had finally opened his heart to someone. Found a connection outside of work.

He would not let Bridget down. He could not…

A hint of a long-forgotten plea whispered across his brain. A prayer a Sunday school teacher had taught him back when his mother was sober enough to remember it was Sunday. He had admired Bridget's faith through all of this.

Have a little faith…

Zach slid out his gun. He stalked toward the rustling in the field. He paused. The sound stopped. "DEA. Show yourself."

Liddie's tearstained face peered around the base of a tree where she had been hiding. "I thought you were him," she said, bracing her hand on the bark and pulling herself to her feet.

"Are you alone?" Zach asked, constantly scanning the area.

"Yah." The single word came out on a squeak.

He tucked his gun back into its holster and rushed

through the tall weeds toward Liddie, extending his hand to help steady her. "Where's Bridget?"

"He has her. He has her." Liddie's panicked gaze bounced around the overgrown field. One cheek had an angry red bruise.

"Are you okay?"

She nodded hesitantly.

"You're safe," Zach reassured her. If only he could say the same about Bridget. He plowed a hand through his hair. "Who has her? The guy from the pool back at Bridget's apartment?"

Liddie narrowed her gaze in confusion. "*Yah*, it was him. I thought Jimmy liked me." She looked up at him with terror in her eyes. Her lower lip quivered.

"He's involved with whatever's going on at the clinic. He was caught on surveillance."

Liddie swung her hand in the direction of the field. "He tossed her phone out there. We need to find it."

"Okay." Zach grabbed his phone. He called Bridget's number. Something caught his eye. He pushed the tall stalks aside with his foot until he reached the muddy tire tracks. His number displayed on a cracked screen.

He picked it up. "Got it."

Liddie held out her hands for the phone, her only connection to her missing sister.

"Let's get you in the truck."

Even though it was a warm summer day, Liddie wrapped her arms around her midsection and shivered. Clumps of partially dried mud clung to the knees of her pants.

"You're going to be okay," Zach reassured her. "We're going to find your sister." He closed the passenger-side door and jogged around to his side of the truck. His pulse whooshed in his ears, reminding him that every fleeting second was another that Bridget was in danger. He yanked open his door and climbed in. "Was he driving a metallic blue muscle car?" He thought about the last photo Bridget had sent him.

Liddie nodded. "It's really loud."

"Tell me what happened. Did Jimmy mention anyone else? A location?" She kept shaking her head. He pulled out onto the country road and kept his eyes peeled for a vehicle that met that description, any sign of Bridget. He feared the kid had a good ten-minute head start.

Liddie retold the story of how she had befriended Jimmy when she had hung around the pool whenever Bridget was at work. They kept in touch by text. When she tried to explain why she had done what she had done, he gently touched her hand. "I'm not judging you. What we have to focus on now is finding your sister."

"He shoved her in the trunk. She's going to die and it's all my fault." Liddie's growing hysteria was frazzling his nerves. He prided himself on his cool demeanor in a crisis, so his growing agitation was disconcerting. He found himself saying another prayer for Bridget's well-being.

"I'll find her." Driving around here aimlessly was wasting time. "I'm going to make a few phone calls." His supervisor had probably had time to run the plate from the photo. "Now that we have more information, we might be able to figure out where he's hiding."

Liddie sniffed back her tears.

"I'm taking you to the hospital." He tightened and loosened his grip on the steering wheel.

"*Neh*, I'm fine." She gingerly touched her cheek. "It's just bruised. Take me home."

"Are you sure?"

Liddie nodded. "You have to find Bridget."

"Okay, okay… Now tell me, did Jimmy mention any names? Anything?"

Liddie stiffened and sat upright. She tapped her leg, as if the memory needed a moment to shake free. "He was screaming at Bridget." Her voice cracked. "He mentioned a Ralphie." She nodded. "*Yah*, a Ralphie." She shrugged, appearing frail and tiny in the passenger seat. "I don't know if that will help."

"Every little bit helps." Zach pulled into her driveway. "Go on in. I'll find Bridget."

Liddie pressed her hands to her cheeks. "I've made a mess of everything. I led him right to her."

Her brothers emerged from the barn and started running toward his truck. "I have to go. Reassure your brothers."

"We need our sister back." Liddie paused at the open passenger door.

"Stay calm. Have your family gather in the house and lock the doors until I get word back to you."

"What am I supposed to say?" Liddie plucked at her T-shirt with a dirty hand.

"The truth." His nerves hummed. He needed to go. "Everything will be okay," he added calmly.

Liddie gave him a watery smile. "You're good for my sister. Maybe when this is all over, you can start courting."

Zach laughed; he couldn't help himself. "Courting, huh? Yeah, I'd like that." His job wouldn't make that easy.

The two brothers reached the truck. "Where were you?" Caleb asked. "Where's Bridget? She went looking for you. *Dat*'s really mad."

"Hold on." Liddie held up her hand to her brother's barrage of questions. "My phone is in Jimmy's car. How will you reach me?"

"I'll reach you," he promised. He started to back out the lane when Jeremiah emerged from his little house.

Zach flicked his hand in a wave, and the two men nodded in silent understanding. He'd allow Liddie to give her
grandfather an update, but he had to make some calls.
See if he could get a hit on this Ralphie guy. Bridget's
life depended on it.

SEVENTEEN

Bridget didn't know what was worse: the blackness, the dank smell, the cramp in her side or her rioting thoughts crashing over her.

I don't want to die. I don't want to die. Please, God, don't let me die.

Sweat trickled down her forehead. Something dull and hard pressed into her hip. No amount of shifting relieved the pressure. It didn't help that her arms were bound behind her. A nagging ache radiated out from where her shoulder supported her weight. She blinked rapidly, unable to see. Panic threatened to overwhelm her. She had to focus, stay clearheaded. Images of all the things he might do to her crowded in on her.

Relax. Be calm.

Jimmy seemed to be driving forever. She didn't know if this was good or bad. She dreaded the moment he stopped. She feared he never would.

Help me. Help me. Help me.

The only peace that kept her from letting a scream rip from her throat was that her sister had gotten away. She only hoped Zach had followed the GPS location of her phone and found her sister. The GPS tracker had been her last hope.

Tears burned the back of her eyes. The throbbing in her cheek had dulled. Growing up Amish, she had been warned countless times to avoid the evils of the outside world. In her naivety, she assumed not following the *Ordnung* would be her downfall, not being stuffed into someone's trunk.

Please help me, Lord. Please...

The car made a sharp turn, and Bridget rolled against the wall of the tight space. A pain ripped through her shoulder. Something damp squished in her fingers. The plastic cut into her wrists. The car bumped over something. The car stopped, then inched forward. The engine cut off. Her heart raced. The sound of something rattled overhead.

The car door opened. Slammed closed.

Breathless anticipation made her dizzy.

Footsteps. A key fob chirp. The click of the trunk release.

Bridget gulped in the fresh air that was tinged with a whiff of exhaust. Her relief was short-lived. Jimmy reached in and yanked her out of the trunk. She blinked against a bright yellow fluorescent light. They were in a garage. An *Englisch* garage with large red toolboxes, motorcycles and folded lawn chairs.

"Please let me go—I won't say anything," Bridget pleaded.

Jimmy laughed. "Too late, sister wife." He was having a good time mocking her. "You should have kept your mouth shut to begin with."

Bridget wondered what he was going to do with her next, but the words got trapped in her throat. Maybe it was better if she didn't know. Nothing good could come from this.

Jimmy grabbed her by her ponytail and led her into the house. Every time she tripped over her feet, he ripped a few more hairs out of her aching scalp. Her heart raced, and her vision tunneled.

Jimmy shoved her down on the couch next to a thin young woman who seemed only vaguely concerned with her sudden arrival. The girl seemed to be watching them through a haze.

"Where's Ralphie?" Jimmy barked at the girl.

"Ralphie?" she said dreamily.

Apparently disgusted with the girl's drug-induced confusion, Jimmy picked up a rope and threw it at her. The girl grunted and swiped at it. "Stop it!"

"Tie her up. Now!" Jimmy's nostrils flared.

The girl smirked and tilted her head lazily toward Bridget. "Her hands are already tied up."

"Unless you want her running out of here, you better find a way to tie her to something."

The girl's face twisted in annoyance. "You do it."

Bridget frantically scanned the room. Jimmy blocked the door. And she'd never be able to lift the window without his violent reaction—or her hands. The back of her head was still throbbing from when he yanked her ponytail. *Don't give up so easily. Maybe there's an exit.* Her gaze drifted to the arched doorway leading to a small front foyer. Blooms of brown water stains covered the ceiling.

Jimmy must have read her mind, because he grabbed Bridget by the arm and tossed her from the couch to the ground. She bit back a yelp when her hip slammed into the hardwood floor and her shoulder into the radiator. Every inch of her body ached, but that paled in comparison to the rioting fear scrambling her thoughts and sending a million pinpricks tightening her tingling skin.

Jimmy snatched the rope from the couch where the young woman had flung it. Bridget struggled to roll over, sit up, but before she had a chance, he kicked her back down. Her breath whooshed out of her. He lunged toward her, grabbed her ankle and dragged her against the radiator under the window. He worked quickly and tied her to the radiator.

Jimmy yanked on the rope to make sure it was secure. The plastic of the zip tie cut into her wrists. She clenched her jaw. He leaned in close and gave her a smile that made her blood run cold. "You're going to be a good girl, right?"

Heat washed over Bridget's face and she nodded, not trusting her voice.

"Ralphie wants to see you himself." He patted her cheek with his open palm. "Wants to make sure I have the right girl this time." He tilted his head, as if reasoning with himself.

"You didn't mean to kill Ashley?" Bridget finally found her voice.

"Ralphie told me I made a big mess. Your death might have been written off as wrong place, wrong time, but two suspicious deaths, especially when you worked together, wouldn't look so hot." He peeled his lips back from his teeth making a sucking noise. "I figured I did him a favor. I found the DEA business card in her apartment when I followed her home." Still crouched down next to her, he scratched his jaw. "I tried to make it look like she packed up and took off, but she was a fighter. Killed her, took her car and dumped her where I watched her jog." He dragged a rough finger down her cheek and she squirmed with nowhere to go. "Even found a way to call in a vacation day so no one would come looking for her right away." He was obviously pleased with himself.

Bridget took shallow breaths, trying to focus as the walls grew close. He had been stalking them. Over his shoulder, the girl seemed out of it.

"So…" He pushed to his feet. "I'm gonna see that you keep your mouth shut forever."

Jimmy grabbed a gun from the side table. Bridget bit back a yelp and he gave her an ugly smile. "Don't worry. Ralphie wants to chat a bit first. Then I get to hurt you."

"You don't have to do this," Bridget pleaded. "Please."

Jimmy shook his head and rolled his eyes. "Your boss should have considered the people he was getting involved with."

Bridget's pulse roared in her ears. "How did you meet Dr. Ryan? I don't understand how he got messed up in all this."

"Far as I know, the doctor had a son with a gambling problem. A very big problem with some very bad people. Started off simply enough. Sell drugs. Make cash. Pay off the loans. Easy to get sucked in, though. Like gambling, I suppose. Not so easy to get out. Turns out, the world is filled with lots of bad people."

Bridget drew in a deep breath and blinked slowly. "Did you kill the doctor in jail?"

Jimmy narrowed his gaze and something sparked in his cycs. He enjoyed all of this. "You ask too many questions." He set the gun on the table next to the girl and said, "Shoot her if she moves, but don't kill her." He locked eyes with Bridget. "I'll be right back." His even tone belied the evil swirling in the dark pools of his eyes. A shiver raced up her spine. This man was broken.

Bridget tracked Jimmy until he slammed the front door and the dead bolt clicked. Her shoulders ached at the awkward angle her body was contorted in, bound to the radiator. She turned her attention to the girl on the couch, who was focusing on the gun. She petted it as if it were a kitty seeking attention. The drugged-out girl's detached manner made Bridget's entire body tremble. Something was seriously wrong with this girl. Bridget's insides twisted at the thought that this intoxicated person was her only hope.

Bridget forced a smile. "Please untie me. He's going to kill me." She didn't mince words. "Please."

The girl playfully fingered the gun, the smooth metal twirling easily on the wooden surface. "What did you do to tick off Ralphie?" she asked without lifting her eyes from the gun.

"I'm a nurse at a health-care clinic. I reported some prescription discrepancies." Bridget decided to try the truth.

The girl's gaze finally landed on Bridget. "Why?"

"Because it was the right thing to do." Bridget tried to shift her shoulders, but nothing would relieve the pain.

"That was dumb." The girl laughed. She stopped playing with the gun and reached into the side table.

Bridget's stomach threatened to revolt. She closed her eyes and said a prayer.

She didn't know how much longer she could hold on to hope.

Zach, come find me.

Zach worked the phone while he raced toward Buffalo. His gut told him this guy was taking Bridget to his home territory. His phone buzzed. It was his ASAC.

"Ma'am," he said into the phone.

"Where are you?"

"Headed back to Buffalo."

"Okay, good. We tied the license plate from the photo Bridget sent you to James Demmer." The guy Zach recognized in the surveillance photos.

"Address?"

"Sent an agent there. His mother hasn't seen him in weeks. Zach…" She seemed to be weighing her words carefully. "He's affiliated with one of the most violent gangs in Buffalo."

A knot fisted in his gut. Not the kind of information he wanted confirmed. "We need a list of their stash houses." *Stay focused*.

"Zach, I think you should get back to the office. I have agents on this. We'll find Bridget."

"But—"

"You're too involved with this case. Come in. You can work it from behind the desk. I can hear the emotion in your voice."

Zach drummed his fingers on the steering wheel. "Colleen…"

"Listen, you've been fully cleared to come back to work next week. You don't want to do anything to mess that up."

"I've got to find her."

"I know, I know. We'll find her. You need to come in."

Zach was about to protest when his ASAC added, "I was going to wait to share the report with you next week. They finished the investigation into Kevin Pearson's death."

"Oh…" His heart thrummed like molasses through his veins.

"Turns out your confidential informant was working both sides. He was relaying information back to his bosses."

"He knew how dangerous that was," Zach said in disbelief. "I warned him."

"Pearson went against everything you had told him. His death, although unfortunate, is not your fault."

Zach scrubbed a hand across his face. "I should have had a better read on the kid. If I hadn't recruited him as an informant—"

"His brother told one of our agents that he mocked your advice." Zach could imagine his supervisor shaking her head. "Kevin was reckless. In light of this, you're cleared to go back into the field."

"Undercover? Great, great." The traffic in front of him slowed.

"You'll come in to the office. I've got Frank on this. As soon as we pull up any potential locations on James Demmer and this Ralphie character, we'll send in a team. I promise."

Silence stretched across the line. "You're too invested in this. Report to headquarters. You hear me?" Colleen asked.

"I hear you." He went to change lanes, and a car honked at him. "Traffic is getting heavy. I need to go."

Zach ended the call and counted to five, then called Special Agent Frank Levy.

"I figured I'd be hearing from you," Frank said by way of greeting.

"What do you have?" Zach didn't bother with the formalities.

"Lots of our agents are out in the field getting eyes on any of the known stash houses of the BFLO gang."

"Jimmy's part of the BFLO gang? You're sure?" Zach's scalp tightened. *Not good.* He had hoped his supervisor's intel had been wrong. They were an especially violent gang. He kept tapping the brake, riding the bumper of the car in front of him. *Get over, get over, get over...*

"Yeah. And we found a Ralphie, a Ralph Booth. He's got ties to two addresses in Buffalo. We've got eyes on both." Frank's phone cut out. "Hold up. One of the agents is calling in."

The car in front of Zach finally got over. He put the pedal all the way down and raced toward Buffalo. His job might be in jeopardy if he didn't follow the ASAC's orders.

His career wouldn't mean much if he couldn't save Bridget.

Frank came back on the line. "One of our agents spotted Jimmy coming out of a house on Lisbon Avenue." He rattled off the house number.

"Was he alone? Do they have eyes on him?"

"Yes and yes. Our guy's following him. No sign of Bridget Miller."

"Is she in the house?" Zach entered the address into his GPS.

"We don't know. A police officer is watching the house in an undercover car. He'll report any action on the house. We'll get a warrant."

"I'm headed there."

"Gotcha." If Frank knew Zach had orders to come straight to the office, he didn't say. Working in a tight-knit group had some perks. They each covered the other's backs.

Zach ended the call and floored it. The GPS said he'd arrive in twenty minutes.

As long as no one got in his way, he'd be there in fifteen. Or less.

EIGHTEEN

Bridget's shoulders ached from the awkward position with her arms tethered to the radiator. The girl on the couch was more interested in searching for split ends than listening to Bridget's reasons as to why she didn't deserve to be held captive.

Bridget prayed that Zach could track her down. *Somehow.*

"What's your name?" Bridget asked.

"Heather," she said almost automatically before glancing up, annoyed, as if Bridget had tricked her into something.

"Do you live here? Or is this Jimmy's house?" She needed a thread of hope that Zach could track her to this address.

The girl harrumphed. "Stop asking questions."

Bridget changed tactics. "My family is going to be worried about me."

The girl's head snapped up, and her slack features contorted in anger. Instinctively, Bridget yanked on the rope. It wouldn't budge. "My family are a bunch of jerks. They don't care about me."

A sharp cramp stabbed her between the shoulder blades. She sucked in a quick breath, then tried to relax her muscles. "Sometimes I think my family doesn't care about me, either." The words came out of her mouth before she had a chance to consider their effect.

The girl's brow furrowed. "You brought it on yourself when you decided to be a tattletale."

"I thought I was doing the right thing." Bridget would have shrugged if she thought it wouldn't hurt. "I'm a nursing student. I want to put this all behind me."

"Boo-hoo," Heather mocked her. Then she picked up a couch pillow and hugged it. "Jimmy said he had to make a trip to Hickory Lane." She got a faraway look in her eyes. "I went there once with my grandma. Bunch of Amish there."

"I'm Amish," Bridget offered, hoping to somehow make a connection with the girl. "I mean, I grew up Amish."

"Really?" The single word came out on a laugh of disbelief. "What are you, on that *Rumspringa*?"

"Well…" Bridget grimaced. "Any chance you could untie me? My arms are killing me."

"Yeah…nope." The girl reached over and grabbed a small kit from the table and popped it open. Bridget couldn't see what it was.

"So, you and your grandma visited Hickory Lane?" Bridget tried to draw the girl back into conversation.

"Yeah…" Heather blinked slowly a few times. "I can't believe you guys don't have TVs. What do you do at night?" Her words were slurred.

"Read. Quilt." Bridget scooted back in a useless attempt to relieve the tension on her shoulders and arms.

The girl shook her head and twisted her lips. She reached into the kit propped open on the pillow and produced a syringe. Bridget's stomach twisted. For the briefest of moments, she thought Heather was going to inject her with something. Instead, the young woman grabbed a band and wrapped it around her own arm.

"Please don't do that," Bridget pleaded. "There's places you can get help." She studied the girl's face. She seemed to pause a moment before putting one end of the band into her mouth and pulling it tight with the other. The girl prepared the drug, filled the needle, then plunged it into her arm. Bridget's heart ached.

All of Heather's features slackened, her eyes closed and her head fell back on the couch. A single tear tracked down Bridget's face. Despair filled her heart despite her prayers.

Bridget wasn't sure how much time had passed. She had begun to doze when a gurgling noise jostled her awake. The girl was slumped to one side and choking on her own vomit. Bridget yanked on her tethered arms. Pain and panic sliced through her. This girl was going to die.

"Help! Help!" Bridget screamed.

A moment later a key sounded in the front door. Jimmy stormed in, his face twisted in anger. He stomped over to Bridget and pressed his damp palm over her mouth. Nicotine was deep in his pores. "Shut up, you idiot." He jammed her head against the radiator, and a new pain sliced through the back of her head. "Shut up!"

Bridget opened her eyes wide and gestured toward the couch behind him. She made an unintelligible sound against his grubby hand. Seeming to sense something else was going on, Jimmy dropped his hand and spun around. "Heather!"

Her eyes were closed. She convulsed and foamed at the mouth.

He tapped her face. "Wake up, wake up, wake up." His frantic tone was in sharp contrast to his evil persona. "Oh, you stupid girl." Jimmy spun around. "She's choking!" He straightened and clasped his hands behind his neck and paced. "This is bad. This is bad. Ralphie's gonna be mad."

Bridget stuffed down her anger. He was more concerned about himself than the poor girl on the couch. "Jimmy! Jimmy!" she said sharply. "Stop. Look at me."

The man stopped midstride and glared at her. "Shut up. I can't think."

"I can help her. You need to untie me."

Jimmy scrubbed a hand across his face. "Shut up."

"She's going to aspirate if you don't help her. If you don't want to untie me, you help her. I'll tell you what to do." The intermittent coughs and sputters from the young woman assured Bridget that she was still breathing. "Put her on the hard floor. Turn her on her side…"

When Jimmy made no effort to move, Bridget said more forcefully, "You have to act now!"

Jimmy took a step toward the girl, then pivoted back toward her. "You know what to do?"

"Yes."

Indecision played on his features, then gave way. Dropping to his knees, he yanked at the knots that had grown tighter with her struggle. He reached behind him and pulled a knife out of a sheath on his belt. He sawed the rope, then the zip tie. Bridget's numb arms fell heavily.

She pushed to her feet and nearly collapsed because her right foot was asleep. "Move her to the floor." She rubbed her wrists vigorously to get blood flowing again.

Jimmy did as he was told, suddenly more concerned about someone other than Bridget. And himself. He set the girl down on the hardwood floor. Bridget crawled over to her and turned her on her side. She hesitated for a fraction. In an ideal situation she'd wash her hands, but a little dirt was the least of this poor girl's concern. She swept out Heather's mouth to clear her airway.

"Is she breathing?" Jimmy asked, hovering over Bridget's shoulder.

A flash of his humanity shone in his eyes. How did people go so wrong?

Bridget checked on her patient. "Yes, she's breathing… you need to keep a close eye on her. Or take her to the hospital."

Jimmy's eyes darted toward the door, then back at her. "That's exactly what you'd want, isn't it?"

Bridget sat back on her heels. "I don't want any of this."

His mouth twitched. Before he could lash out at her, a pounding sounded on the front door. Jimmy cursed. He stomped toward the front door and pulled back the heavy curtain on one of the sidelights to peek out. He unbolted the door, and another man came in. The subtle bow of Jimmy's head made it clear who was in charge. The man took in the scene. "What's going on here?"

Jimmy seemed to take in the situation, too. Bits of vomit were tangled in the girl's long hair that was splayed across the hardwood floor. Her leg was bent at an awkward angle.

Jimmy didn't need to answer for the man to come to his own conclusions. "You need to get her out of here."

Bridget straightened her back. "This girl needs to go to the hospital."

A slow slant curved the man's lips, making a cold chill skitter up her spine. "Ah, Bridget… You should be more concerned about yourself."

Bridget scooted away until her back was pressed against the couch. The man approached her menacingly.

The doorbell rang, and the man's head snapped up and found Jimmy. "You expecting someone?" His jaw gritted and his fist came up. "So help me…" He reached for the gun.

"No, no," Jimmy said, obviously agitated. "Ralphie, you have to believe me. I didn't tell anyone where we were."

So, this is Ralphie.

Ralphie raised a skeptical eyebrow at Jimmy. He pulled back the curtain and waved his gun at them behind his back. "Keep your mouths shut." The man yanked open the door. "What?"

"I was looking for Jimmy. He told me I could stop by for..." The man outside coughed. "Man, maybe I have the wrong house."

A concerned expression pinched Jimmy's features as he watched the front door. Just then the man who had knocked on the door exploded through the opening and shoved Ralphie against the wall. Ralphie's gun dropped with a clatter. Another officer swept in and grabbed Ralphie and rushed him out of the house. Jimmy snagged the gun and grabbed Bridget's ponytail—ugh, her ponytail—and pulled her head back before the remaining officer had a chance to get her to safety.

"Please," she pleaded. "Let me go!"

Another crash sounded from the back of the house. Jimmy turned 180, his eyes wide.

Jimmy lifted the gun to her temple. He pivoted and put her body between him and whoever was coming through the back door. He swung around to face the other officer near the front door.

Help me, Lord.

Zach burst into the tight quarters with his gun drawn. Bridget's relief was tempered by the forearm cutting off her airflow and the cool barrel of a gun pressed into her temple.

"Step away before I take off your head," Zach growled.

Jimmy tightened his hold around Bridget's neck. "No way."

Zach nodded to the other officer, who quietly backed out the front door. "It's just you and me. Let her go."

Had all her decisions—to turn her back on the *Ordnung*, to leave her family, to get an education against her father's wishes—led to this?

Zach trained his gun on the punk who held Bridget. Her eyes radiated her panic as she clawed at the arm around her neck. His pulse deafened him at the thought of Bridget being hurt. Or worse.

"Let her go," he commanded. He continued his slow and steady advance.

The kid's eyes flared wide and moved rapidly. "Stay back or I'm going to kill her."

"No one's gonna die today," Zach reasoned, holding one hand out and the other on his gun carefully trained on the kid's head. "If anything happens to either of these women, I think your boss, who's currently getting tucked into the back seat of a police cruiser, will be more than interested to hear how you cooperated in this investigation. How you led the DEA right to his doorstep."

Jimmy's head swiveled as if on a stick. "I did not. I did not."

Zach shrugged casually, cautiously ratcheting up the kid's paranoia.

"If you put that information out there, I'm as good as dead," the kid said, his expression anguished.

Zach made eye contact with Bridget. She struggled to loosen the grip around her neck. Her face had grown red. Zach nodded ever so slightly, indicating that she needed to trust him. She blinked slowly in acknowledgment.

"Let her go now or there's no negotiating." Zach inched closer.

"They'll get to me in prison. Ralphie's got people everywhere." The kid's complexion had grown a deathly white. *Like they got to the doctor.*

"Let her go and maybe I can arrange witness protection. Keep you safe."

The kid's gaze slid to Zach's. The slight arch of his brow suggested he might be considering it.

"Come on," Zach coaxed, taking another step closer. "This is your last chance. Come on." He held out his palm for the gun, and that was the final encouragement the kid needed. His shoulders sagged, and he handed over his gun. In Jimmy's last act of defiance, he pushed Bridget toward him. Zach caught her, careful to hold the guns away from her. "I got you. Are you okay?"

Bridget rubbed her throat and nodded.

Zach gently sat her down on the couch, nearly tripping over the young woman on the floor. Jimmy plowed through the kitchen chairs on the way toward the back of the house.

"Give me your phone. I have to call an ambulance. And you need to go catch him," Bridget said, her voice raspy.

He tucked a strand of Bridget's hair behind her ear, knowing there was an officer guarding the back door. "I'll be right back." He straightened and strolled toward the back of the house. In the overgrown yard, he found Jimmy facedown on the driveway. Zach's friend Officer Freddy Mack was taking him into custody.

"You looking for this guy?" Freddy stood and yanked up the kid by the handcuffs. His head lolled forward in complete defeat.

"Thanks for covering the back."

Freddy gave him a subtle nod. The law enforcement agencies had worked well together to combat the drug trade. "I'll take this guy in."

"Thanks." Zach turned toward the house. The green

paint had bubbled and peeled. An ambulance sounded in the distance. "I'll meet you downtown." Zach rushed into the house, anxious to see Bridget, to convince himself that she really was okay. Already the self-recriminations were pinging in his brain. He never should have left her alone in Hickory Lane. She could have been killed.

Back in the house, he found Bridget kneeling on the floor next to the unconscious girl, checking her vitals. A few minutes later, the paramedics bumped their stretcher through the small entryway. Zach crouched down next to Bridget. "Come on," he whispered. "The paramedics are here. You've done everything you can. And I'm going to drive you to the ER myself. Tell me what hurts."

A faraway look glistened in her eyes. He placed his hand on her back and helped her stand. "Come on." He guided her toward the door. Her attention drifted back toward the girl. "Her name's Heather. That's all I know. She injected the drugs from that kit on the couch. Her pulse is thready. She was vomiting."

One of the paramedics nodded. "We'll take good care of her." He set his medical kit down next to the young woman and began working on her.

Zach led Bridget outside to his truck. She spun around to face him. "Liddie! Is she okay?"

"Yes, she's fine. She's home."

Her eyes turned watery with relief. "So, you got my texts?"

"Yes." He planted a kiss on the crown of her head, then pulled back to meet her gaze. "You're one smart woman."

A smile slanted her pretty pink lips.

He gave himself a mental shake. He had to make sure she was okay. "Come here." He opened the passenger door of his truck and had her sit down. He cupped her face with his hand, examining her tender cheek. The skin under one eye was bruised. "What did he do to you?" He found himself holding his breath, fearful of what had happened when he couldn't protect her.

Bridget told him how Liddie had been in contact with Jimmy, ultimately leading him to her. How he stuffed her into the trunk and drove her here. How he tied her to the radiator and only let her go to help the girl who had overdosed. Bridget struck him as both calm and relieved. She was one impressive woman.

"Let's get you to the hospital." Zach's gaze traveled the length of her. "I should have been there for you."

She blinked a few times, then smiled up at him. "You were." She reached out and grabbed a handful of his shirt and pulled him close. "You were." She stretched up and kissed him. The warmth of her lips, the smell of her skin, her solid presence soothed the adrenaline that had been coursing through his veins.

Thank You, Lord.

When had he ever said a prayer in gratitude? Inwardly he smiled. Bridget had influenced him in more ways than one.

The fresh breeze cooled Bridget's fiery cheeks as she swung her legs again into the vehicle. Her fingers brushed across her lips, surprised at her boldness. He smiled at her again. "We should get you to the hospital," he said, resting his strong hand on her knee.

"I'm fine. Really." She rubbed her raw wrists.

"I'd feel better if you were examined by a doctor."

Bridget smiled and reached up for the seat belt. Oh, she was going to be sore tomorrow.

Tomorrow. Did all this mean that tomorrow her life

would go back to normal? Just like that? Doubt niggled at her.

Zach stepped back to close the door when he paused and said, "What's that look for?"

"I was thinking. Does this mean I can go back to my normal life?" Where would she stay? Would she be able to catch up with her classes? What about her family? She rubbed her forehead, holding back the myriad of questions. After all, they weren't Zach's problems. He was officially off the hook. The bad guys had been arrested, and she was still on this side of heaven.

"I don't see why not. We'll want to make sure there's no lingering players still running around..." he nodded as if convincing himself "...yeah, you can go back to your life."

"I'll have to find a place to live." Bridget lifted her hand. "I'll figure it out. I always have."

Something flashed in the depths of his eyes, and he opened his mouth, then snapped it shut. "You ready?"

"I'll need to get my stuff and say goodbye to my family and friends in Hickory Lane, too." She couldn't slip away in the dead of night this time.

"Of course. I can take you back after you're checked out at the hospital. I'm sure one of the police officers can take your statement while we're there."

Bridget crossed her arms and shivered. The air had grown chilly. "I can't deal with my family tonight."

"Whatever you need."

"Maybe I could find a cheap motel?" She ran her pinkie over the tender skin under her eye.

"I have a better idea."

"Oh?" Her stomach pitched.

"My mother's house is a few blocks away. I don't think she'd mind putting you up."

Bridget frowned. "I thought you were estranged. I don't want to cause any problems."

"I stopped by her house." He seemed to be considering something. "I think she wouldn't mind." One shoulder tipped up slightly. "Can't hurt to ask."

"If you think she wouldn't mind." She rubbed her palms on her jeans.

He tilted his head. "Should we go?"

Before she had a chance to reply, their attention was drawn to the paramedics carrying out Heather on a stretcher. "Hold on." Bridget released the seat belt and scooted out of the truck, brushed by Zach and walked gingerly over to the back of the ambulance. Heather had on an oxygen mask, and her eyes were open. "Is she going to be okay?"

"Yeah. This time." The paramedic's resigned tone suggested he had seen it all. The girl would recover tonight, but what about the next time? Unfortunately, that's all the assurance he could give Bridget.

She met Heather's gaze for a brief moment before the doors slammed shut and the driver rushed past her. Bridget stared after the ambulance as it pulled out of the driveway without lights or sirens. Perhaps Heather was going to be okay. And maybe Bridget had played a small role in that.

"You ready?" Zach said, placing his hand on the small of her back.

Bridget took comfort in his touch as they made their way back to the truck. A small crowd had gathered on the sidewalk across the street, gawking at the excitement on Lisbon Avenue. People were fascinated by other people's misery. People's lives ruined because of their drug addiction. Tragedy narrowly avoided. Cautionary tales?

Any doubt that Bridget had made the wrong decision to report the illegal drug activity at the clinic that, in turn, had upended her life had disappeared the moment the ambulance doors had slammed shut. She could never sit idly by.

Bridget exhaled sharply. "Yeah, I'm ready."

EPILOGUE

Nine months later

Downstairs among all the other graduates at University at Buffalo's Alumni Arena, Bridget straightened her mortarboard and her shoulders. She'd made it. She had actually made it.

It had taken a few weeks to catch up on her fall classes, but her professors were supportive. Her living situation had worked out well, too. Zach's friend Freddy Mack and his wife, Jess, had allowed her to rent a room in their home. Since both of them were Buffalo police officers, Bridget felt safe. Now, nine months later, it seemed any repercussions from her involvement in the fraud investigation at the clinic had truly blown over. Both Jimmy and Ralphie would be spending the foreseeable future in prison for their roles in the drug trade, Ashley's death and the near misses on Bridget's life. And sadly, Dr. Seth Ryan had lost his life over his part.

So many lives ruined.

Last Bridget heard, Heather had successfully finished rehab and Bridget prayed the young woman from the stash house stayed sober. Any of Bridget's efforts to reach out to the Ryan family had been met with silence. Hopefully, the doctor's son had given up gambling and could live with the horrible consequences of his actions.

Fortunately for the residents of one corner of the Buffalo community, the health-care clinic had reopened under a small group of physicians who rotated through. Bridget had felt great relief at that. Maybe she'd volunteer her time there—or at another clinic that served those most in need—once she got settled in her new nursing career. She still kept kicking around the idea of continuing her studies. Maybe become a nurse practitioner.

Excitement bubbled to the surface at all the possibilities.

A girl approached her. "Are these the *M*s?" The graduates were lined up alphabetically.

"Yes, I'm Miller."

"Oh, good. Milliken here." The girl tugged on her honors rope and stepped into line behind Bridget, who found herself scanning the line of graduates ahead of her. Her friend Ashley Meadows should have been somewhere in front of her... She shook away the thought. Poor Ashley.

The graduation coordinator clapped her hands above the din to get their attention. The soon-to-be alumni quieted down, and the graduates began the procession up the stairs to the auditorium.

Zach met the passenger van in the loop outside the arena. He had told Bridget he'd do his best to attend her graduation, cautioning her that he might get stuck at work. He had been busy in yet another undercover assignment, but he wouldn't miss this day for the world.

Over the past school year, he and Bridget had grown close, squeezing in dates between schoolwork and undercover assignments. They filled the time between with texts. They kept talk of the future to a minimum, fearing his undercover work would never allow for a normal life.

The past nine months had changed him in ways he never imagined. He had fallen hard for the beautiful woman from Hickory Lane, and he suspected—no, he prayed— the feeling was mutual.

The van driver slowed, and Zach waved. The man tipped his chin and pulled over beyond the blue crosswalk. The side door popped open, and Bridget's family climbed out: Liddie, Elijah, Caleb, Jeremiah, Mae and Amos. Bridget's father had been especially hard to convince to attend his daughter's graduation. Zach had a feeling her grandfather Jeremiah had had a hand in his presence.

Zach enjoyed watching Caleb and Elijah take in the campus with slack-jawed expressions under their felt hats.

"Well," Zach said, holding out his hand toward the arena, "the ceremony is about to start. We better go in."

Zach ushered them into the arena to curious glances. When a recording of "Pomp and Circumstance" sounded over the speakers, the audience shifted their attention to the processing graduates, hoping to spot their loved ones.

Bridget's parents sat quietly while Caleb and Elijah pointed out things and discussed them between themselves. Liddie leaned over to Zach and asked if he thought she should go to college. Zach smiled, not daring to cause any waves. On the other side of him, Jeremiah whispered, "Thanks for inviting us."

"Thanks for convincing everyone to come."

Jeremiah nodded.

After Bridget walked across the stage and made it back to her seat—Zach was able to watch her from the nose-bleeds—he texted her with a bunch of celebratory emojis. Then he typed, You did it! Congrats!

Three dots appeared on the screen. You're here! Then more bubbles. I can't believe you spotted me in this crowd.

He tapped away with his thumbs. How could I miss

this? You were easy to spot. You're the most beautiful graduate here!

She responded with an "aw shucks" GIF.

He laughed and texted one more time: Meet me outside by the buffalo after the ceremony.

When the recessional music started, excitement coursed through Zach's veins. He patted his suit coat pocket and squared his shoulders.

The audience spilled out into the aisles. Bridget's father's face grew pinched under the shadow of his felt hat. "We can wait a minute until the crowd clears," Zach suggested.

Mae smiled her agreement and patted her husband's arm.

Caleb and Elijah looked like they wanted to hop out of their seats and go exploring. Zach couldn't blame them. Liddie seemed to be taking everything in. He had a hard time reading her. On the one hand, she seemed like the dutiful daughter, but on the other, she seemed to be ready to push the boundaries. Zach supposed that children growing into adults often pushed boundaries, no matter what the culture.

Last year, when he had taken Bridget home to collect her things, he sensed Amos's displeasure with both his daughters. Bridget for her plans to leave again and toward Liddie, perhaps for having kept in communication with Jimmy. Zach hoped they could work it out. He knew the strain of harboring resentment toward a love one.

The crowd began to thin a bit. "Let's head out. I told Bridget I'd meet her outside." He overheard Amos lean in and tell his wife that maybe they should have brought flowers for their daughter, and Mae reassured him that being here was gift enough.

Zach smiled. It seemed that Amos had made peace with at least one of his daughters.

When they reached the exit, the pavement was teeming with people. Zach searched their faces. When his gaze finally landed on Bridget, she was staring in his direction with wide eyes. Apparently, she had spotted her family quicker than he had found her. Perhaps their Amish clothing made them stand out.

She broke through the crowd and into his embrace. He whispered into her hair, "You did it! Congratulations!"

Bridget pulled back quickly and brushed a chaste kiss across his cheek. "Thank you. Thank you for all of this." She clutched her diploma to her chest and turned to her family. "I can't believe you came." Her smile spread from ear to ear. "This means so much more to me with you all here."

"You must get your intelligence from me," her grandfather joked, the first to break the awkward silence.

Her mother smiled proudly but didn't say anything, perhaps taking her cues from Amos, who stood stiffly among the sea of graduates and their families.

"Hey, I heard there was food involved," Liddie spoke up. "I'm starving."

"Of course," Zach said. "I'll call the driver." His gaze touched on each of Bridget's family members before landing on her. "We can all go back to my mother's home for a celebration."

A single tear leaked out of the corner of Bridget's eye as color infused her face. "Thank you," she mouthed. "Thank you so much."

The sun had lowered in the sky, and a late spring chill was in the air. Bridget sat across from her parents at the picnic table in Zach's childhood yard. She couldn't believe Zach and his mother had organized all this.

His mother, Annie, came out with a fresh pitcher of iced tea. "Does anyone need a top off?"

Her father lifted his hand and readied himself to stand. "Thank you for your hospitality. It's time we go. We have a long ride home."

A hint of disappointment swept through Bridget. "Thank you for coming. It meant a lot to me." Her father had been his usual quiet self, but he had been gracious, and she sensed he had made peace with her decision.

Bridget's father stood to leave and she got to her feet to join him. He hesitated, then said, "Don't forget where you came from."

Bridget touched her father's arm. "I won't."

He tipped his hat and strode around the side of the house to the van parked out front.

"'Bye, *Mem*." Bridget pulled her mother into a tight embrace. "Thanks so much for everything."

Her mother seemed to be holding back tears. "Remember what your father told you."

"I will. I will." Her voice cracked, and she caught Zach's warm gaze.

"Well, *denki*. I better catch up to your father. Come on," she said to the rest of her family.

Elijah muttered his goodbyes, and Caleb bowed his head and dived into his sister's side. Bridget bent down and kissed his head. "You boys be good."

Caleb looked up with tears in his eyes. "Will you come visit us?"

Bridget looked toward the side of the house where her parents had gone on their way to the van. She didn't want to lie because she didn't know if she'd be welcomed home on a regular basis.

She locked gazes with Zach, then leaned over and kissed the top of her brother's sweaty head again. "I'll always be here for you." And she meant that. Then she playfully patted his arm. "Better go get into the van. It's a long walk to Hickory Lane."

"You wouldn't make us walk," Caleb said with an air of disbelief.

Bridget playfully hip checked him and laughed. "Don't test me."

The two boys raced each other around the side of the house. Liddie picked up her paper plate of graduation cake and a plastic fork. "Not going anywhere without this."

"Enjoy." Bridget smiled. Zach pulled Bridget close in a side hug.

Liddie took a bite of cake and licked a bit of frosting from her lip. "You will come visit us, right?"

"I'll try." Bridget was more forthright with her sister. "Dad made an exception to come here, but I'm not sure if he'll leave the door open for me to come and go as I please. It wouldn't set a good example." She reached out and squeezed her sister's arm. "I'm here. I'll always be here. You have my phone number." Then she playfully wagged her finger at her sister. "Be *gut*."

Liddie pointed at herself with the fork as if to say, *Who me?* Bridget had asked Liddie about Moses, the man who had courted Bridget years earlier and who had strangely shown up on the day Liddie decided to meet Jimmy. Liddie had dismissed Moses. She claimed he was a nuisance. Nothing more than that. Bridget chose to believe her sister.

"I hope you learned your lesson." Bridget's grandfather stepped outside onto the back porch.

Liddie rolled her eyes. "Listen to the biggest rebel of them all." Apparently, her grandfather's misadventures had become well-known among his granddaughters in light of recent events.

He ran a hand across his beard. "Do as I say, not as I

do." He laughed, then tipped his head at Zach. "Take care of her."

"Yes, sir." Zach squeezed Bridget's shoulders. "Thanks for coming. Let me walk you to the van."

Her grandfather waved him off. "I'm perfectly capable of walking to the van. Come on, Liddie. Our chariot awaits."

"'Bye, Bridget. 'Bye, Zach." Liddie's eyes danced, and she took another bite of her cake and strolled away.

Bridget stepped away from Zach. "Well, I better help your mom clean up."

"No, no." Zach had taken off his suit coat and now he wore only his button-down with rolled-up sleeves. "I've got this. Sit. Relax." He directed her toward a chair on the patio. "The bugs shouldn't bother you here."

Bridget sat and reflected on the day. It was perfect. The sounds of Annie and her grown son talking easily over the running of water and clanking of dishes floated out to her. Their relationship was definitely on the mend.

She tipped her head back and settled into the chair. The scent from the citronella candle tickled her nose. Now that she had her bachelor's degree, she couldn't shake the idea of continuing on to graduate school. She hadn't yet discussed it with Zach. He had insisted she focus on school and not let him distract her. Yet as the months and days passed, she had found she wanted her plans to intertwine with his.

Would that be possible with his job?

A short time later, Zach returned with two iced teas. "Hey there. How's my college graduate?" The pride in his voice warmed her heart.

She took a sip and set the glass on the small table between them. "I start my job at the hospital on Monday." She swallowed hard. "Will you be starting a new assignment soon?" There it was. The thing she had been avoiding all day. How much time could they spend together before he got lost in another undercover assignment?

Zach scooted to the edge of his patio chair and set his drink down next to hers. "Well…" A slow smile played on his lips.

Excitement with underpinnings of apprehension and, if she was being honest, a touch of fear danced across her skin. "What is it?"

"I've spent the past several years undercover." He scrubbed a hand over his hair. "It's been a tough life."

"I can imagine."

"I was offered an assignment at the DEA Training Academy in Quantico. I'm ready for a change."

"Quantico." A fluttering started in her belly. "Where's that? Virginia?" Was he leaving her, too?

"Yes." He seemed to be studying her face. "I was hoping you'd come with me."

Bridget jerked her head back. "I have a job here."

"There are jobs there." He pressed his lips together. "And I know you were considering grad school. There are some fantastic graduate programs in that area."

Had he seen the college brochures at her house?

"I… How?" She couldn't wrap her head around this. Before she had another second to process the details, Zach had slid out of his chair and knelt down on one knee in front of her. He pulled out a box from his suit coat slung over the back of his chair.

"Will you marry me, Bridget Miller?"

She pressed her hands to her cheeks and stared at the ring. "It's so sparkly."

"Is that a yes?" Zach gently pulled her hands away from her face and drew her up into his embrace.

"Yes!" She buried her face in his chest. "Yes."

He took her hand and slipped on the ring. She held it out. "It's beautiful."

He drew a thumb across her cheek. "You're beautiful."

She smiled tightly, and a whisper of sadness threatened to dim this moment. "I wish I could share this with my family."

"We can visit Hickory Lane whenever you want. I promise."

She reached up and gently kissed his lips. "I know you'd do anything for me."

"I want you to know I'll support whatever you decide to do. Grad school. Work. Both." They laughed in unison. "Or if you decide to stay home with our children, I'll support that."

"Children?" Her face grew warm. She hadn't thought that far down the road.

"Yes, children. If you want." His hand brushed across her back, pulling her close. "I'd love to have children with you." He kissed her gently on the lips. "We can figure all that out together."

Bridget planted her left hand on his solid chest and tucked her head under his chin.

"I love you," he whispered into her hair.

"I love you, too." She drew in a deep breath. His subtle aloe aftershave and clean-soap scent reminded her of all the times he had held her like this. Made her feel protected. Loved.

This was home.

He was home.

* * * * *

Look for the next book from Alison Stone,
featuring Bridget's sister, Liddie,
coming later in 2021!

And look for these other Amish titles from
reader favorite Alison Stone:

Plain Protector
Plain Cover-Up
Plain Sanctuary
Plain Jeopardy
Plain Outsider

Available now from Love Inspired Suspense!

Dear Reader,

Thank you for reading *Seeking Amish Shelter*, my first book in a new series set in Hickory Lane, a fictional town in Western New York. When I first started writing books set among the Amish, I learned that there is a large Amish population not too far from my home outside Buffalo. So now all my books are set within a short driving distance from my hometown. Fortunately for me, the real Conewango Valley includes a wonderful candy store with yummy chocolate-covered pretzels. (I think I'm overdue for another research trip!)

In this book, Bridget, who grew up Amish, finds love with an *Englischer*. It's always a delicate balance when I have a character abandon their Amish roots. I try to be respectful of their conservative Christian beliefs while also acknowledging that Christians can be found in all walks of life. And it's a wonderful reminder that in a world where there's a tendency to look for things that divide us, we can just as easily look for things that bring us together.

I hope you'll look for Bridget's sister's story coming from Harlequin Love Inspired Suspense in the future. As soon as I finish this letter, I'll get back to finding mayhem—and love—for Bridget's sister, Liddie.

Hope to see you back in Hickory Lane.

Regards,
Alison

SPECIAL EXCERPT FROM

Among the Amish of River Haven, the past won't stay buried for long…

Read a special excerpt of
Amish Secrets,
*the third book in the River Haven series
by Marta Perry, coming December 2020 from HQN.*

The sound of hammering drew Rachel Hurst around the building, past a thick row of lilacs in full bloom, ranging from deepest purple to pure white. As she rounded the corner of the house, a grape arbor came into view. She stopped, entranced by the memories that seized her.

The grape arbor had been her place, and the pounding was coming from inside it. The gardener, maybe? She certainly hoped it wasn't being torn down.

Walking on, she reached a point at which she could see the inside. She came to a dead stop. Someone was working on the arbor, someone who stopped and stared at her as if he didn't believe what he was seeing.

Fair enough, because she didn't want to believe what she was seeing, either. Jacob Beiler, the one person in the Amish community she didn't want to meet here or anywhere else. Jacob Beiler, the man she'd jilted nearly ten years ago. And he was staring at her with a look cold enough to freeze her on the spot.

***

It took Jacob just a second to recover from the unexpected sight and project the attitude he had maintained toward

Rachel for years—the attitude that had gone a long way toward getting him through glimpses of her at worship or at community events.

Calm, polite acceptance of another member of the Leit—that's all she was to him. At least, that was what he told himself, suppressing the sense of resentment that came without warning.

"Rachel. I didn't expect to see you here." If he had, he'd have been better prepared.

At least he could take pride in the fact that she looked even more affected than he had. He'd have to count that as a point in the odd game of not caring they'd been playing for years.

Rachel straightened, seeming to force a smile. "I didn't, either. Expect to see you, I mean." She nodded toward his toolbox. "You're doing some work here, ain't so?"

She had to know he specialized in the restoration of old houses, a popular trend among the Englisch. She was probably thinking that mending a simple grape arbor was a comedown for him.

Shrugging, he gestured at the arbor. "This is just a little extra job for Ms. Withers. Anyone could fix this. I've been restoring and refinishing the woodwork in the house."

"In the house." She repeated the words as if needing to be sure of them. "I…I didn't know."

Did that mean she wouldn't have been here if she'd known he was? Well, she couldn't be more eager to avoid him than he was to avoid her. The bitterness he'd been trying to conquer for years welled up as fresh as if it had been yesterday. It looked like he had some more work to do on the whole forgive-and-forget idea.

Amish Secrets by Marta Perry.
Coming soon from HQN Books.

HQNBooks.com

PHMPEXP0121